29.99

REDEEMING GRACE

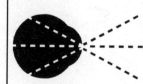

This Large Print Book carries the
Seal of Approval of N.A.V.H.

REDEEMING GRACE

EMMA MILLER

THORNDIKE PRESS
A part of Gale, Cengage Learning

GALE
CENGAGE Learning®

Detroit • New York • San Francisco • New Haven, Conn • Waterville, Maine • London

GALE
CENGAGE Learning·

LIBRARY OF CONGRESS CATALOGING-IN-PUBLICATION DATA

Miller, Emma.
  Redeeming Grace / by Emma Miller.
    pages ; cm. — (Hannah's daughters series) (Thorndike Press large print gentle romance)
  ISBN 978-1-4104-5787-5 (hardcover) — ISBN 1-4104-5787-7 (hardcover)
  1. Amish women—Fiction. 2. Mennonites—Fiction. 3. Large type books. I. Title.
  PS3613.I536R43 2013
  813'.6—dc23
                                           2013004108

Published in 2013 by arrangement with Harlequin Books S.A.

Printed in the United States of America
1 2 3 4 5 6 7 17 16 15 14 13

But by the Grace of God,
I am what I am.
— *1 Corinthians* 15:10

CHAPTER ONE

Kent County, Delaware . . . October
The storm beat against the windows of the house and rattled the glass panes. Since the early hours of morning, the nor'easter had hovered over the state, bringing high gusts of wind that ripped loose shingles on the outbuildings, sent leaves and branches whirling from the big shade trees and dumped torrents of rain over the Yoder farm. It was almost 10:00 p.m., nearly an hour past Hannah's usual bedtime, but she'd lingered in the kitchen, reading from her Bible and listening to Aunt Jezzy sing old German hymns while she knitted by lamplight.

Neither Irwin, Hannah's foster son, nor her two youngest daughters, Susanna and Rebecca, had retired for the night. The young people seemed content to remain in the kitchen, warm and snug, sipping hot cocoa, eating buttered popcorn and playing

Dutch Blitz.

Today had been a visiting Sunday, rather than a day of worship, and so it had been a relaxing day. Usually, on visiting Sundays, Hannah's household would have company over or share the midday meal with one of her married daughters or friends. But the nor'easter had kept everyone home. Simply getting to the barn and chicken house to care for the livestock and poultry had been a struggle.

Footsteps in the hall signaled Johanna's return to the kitchen. Hannah's oldest daughter had taken her two children up to bed earlier and stayed with them, reading aloud and hearing their evening prayers, until they dropped off to sleep. Katie, three, had adjusted easily to the move to her grandmother's house, but Jonah, now five, was still difficult to get in bed, and once there, he was prone to nightmares. Since Johanna and the children had returned to live with Hannah, almost a year and a half ago, the boy often woke the entire house in the middle of the night screaming, and nothing would satisfy him but his mother's arms around him.

"Did you get them down all right?" Hannah asked as Johanna appeared. Hannah thought her daughter looked tired tonight.

The strain of her husband's illness and suicide and the need to return to her mother's home had been hard on her; now she was learning the struggles of being a single mother. Even with the support of her family and friends, it was a difficult time in Johanna's life. Hannah knew that Johanna worried about her son, and prayed that God would ease Johanna's mind.

"Katie was fine, but there's a loose shutter on the bedroom window, and Jonah was afraid that a monster was trying to get in."

Hannah glanced at Irwin suspiciously. Even though he was almost fifteen, he still behaved young for his age, probably as a result of his parents' death and his being shuffled around. "Have you been telling him stories about trolls again?"

Irwin's face reddened and he feigned innocence. "Trolls? Me?"

"Under the corncrib," Susanna supplied, looking up from her cards. She nodded firmly. "*Ya*. You said there was trolls with scabby knees, fleas in their ears and buck teeth."

"Did not," Irwin protested. "Moles. I might have said there was moles under the corncrib."

"*Were* moles," Hannah corrected.

Johanna frowned. "Find someone your

9

own age to tease."

"But I didn't," Irwin insisted, hunching his shoulders. "Must have been one of Samuel's twins who told Jonah that."

"We'll discuss it tomorrow. With Jonah," Hannah said, marking her place in *John* with a red ribbon. She closed the big Bible. "Past time you were in bed, anyway. You'll have to leave early to get to school in time to start a fire in the woodstove. After all this rain, the schoolhouse will be damp."

"Maybe the storm will get worse," Irwin suggested. "Maybe there will be so much rain the school will wash away."

"I doubt that," Johanna said. "It's built on high ground, with a brick foundation."

Reluctantly, Irwin stood up, unfolding his long, gangly legs. He'd grown so much in the past three months that the trousers Hannah had sewn for him in June were already high waters, short even for an Amish teenager. She'd have to see about new clothes for him. Irwin was shooting up faster than a jimson weed.

She'd never regretted taking him in after his parents died in that terrible fire, but an Amish teacher's salary went only so far. Like everyone else, she had to watch her pennies, especially now that Johanna and the children had come back home to live.

10

Not that Johanna was a burden; she contributed as much as she could. She had her sheep, her turkeys and her quilting, as well as the sale of honey from her beehives.

Johanna picked up the empty popcorn bowl and Irwin's mug. "I think I'll turn in now, Mam. I have to finish that quilt for that English lady tomorrow."

"You think you can?" Aunt Jezzy asked. "If it's still raining, Jonah will be stuck inside again all day, and —"

"I know," Johanna agreed. "He has so much energy, he'll be a handful."

"I can take him with me to Anna's," Rebecca offered. "He can play with Mae. The two of them are less trouble when they're together."

"Would you?" Johanna said. "That would be so much help. Katie follows Susanna around like a little shadow, and if you take Jonah for the day, I know I can finish those last few squares and press the quilt in no time. The lady's coming for it Tuesday afternoon."

Irwin went to the kitchen door. "Come on, Jeremiah," he called to his terrier. "Last chance to go out tonight. You, too, Flora." The sheepdog rose off her bed near the pantry and slowly padded after Jeremiah.

Abruptly, a blast of wind caught the

11

screen door and nearly yanked it from Irwin's grasp. He grabbed it with both hands, stepped out onto the porch and then immediately retreated back into the kitchen, tracking rain on the clean floor. Irwin's mouth gaped and he pointed. "There's somethin' . . . somebody . . . Hannah! Come quick!"

Jeremiah's hackles went up, and both dogs began to bark from the doorway.

"What's wrong with you, boy?" Johanna said. "Don't leave the door open. You're believing your own tall tales. Who would be out there on a night like this?"

Hannah tightened her head scarf and hurried to the door as Susanna, now on her feet, let out a gasp and ducked behind Rebecca.

"I don't see —" Hannah began, and then she stopped short. "There *is* someone." She stepped through the open doorway onto the porch.

Standing out on the porch steps was a woman. Hannah sheltered her eyes from the driving rain and raised her voice to be heard above the storm. "Can I help you?" she called, shivering. She couldn't see any vehicles in the yard, but it was so dark that she couldn't be sure there wasn't one.

"Who is it, Mam?" Johanna came out on

12

the porch behind her.

"An English woman," Hannah said. She motioned to the stranger. "Don't stand there. Come in."

Johanna put a restraining hand on her arm. "Do you think it's safe?" she asked in German. Then, in English, she said, "Are you alone?"

The girl shook her head. "I . . . I have my son with me." She turned her head and looked behind her.

Standing on the lower step was one very small, very wet child. Instantly, Hannah's caution receded, and all she could think of was getting the two of them out of the rain, dried off and warmed up. "Come in this moment, both of you," she said. She stood aside, grasping the door, and motioned the English people into the house. Seconds later, they were all standing in the middle of the kitchen, dripping streams of water off their clothing and faces. The young woman was carrying an old guitar case and a stained duffel bag.

For a long moment, there was silence as the Amish and the English strangers stared at each other amid the still-barking dogs. "Hush," Hannah ordered. Flora immediately obeyed, but Jeremiah circled behind Irwin and kept yipping. Hannah clapped her hands. "I said, *be still.*"

This time, the terrier gave a whine and retreated under the table where he continued to utter small growls. And then Susanna broke the awkwardness by grabbing a big towel off the clothesline over the woodstove and wrapping it around the small boy.

"He's wet," Susanna said. "And cold. His teeth are chattering."

"*Ya,* I'm afraid he is cold," Hannah agreed. "Please," she said to the young woman. "You're drenched. Get out of that sweater."

The stranger, her face as pale as skim milk, set down her things and stripped off a torn gray sweater. In the lamplight, Hannah could see that she wasn't as young as she had first thought. Mid-to-late twenties probably. Her cheeks were hollow, and dark shadows smudged the area beneath her tired blue eyes. She was small and thin, the crown of her head barely coming to Johanna's shoulder. But her face in no way prepared them for the very odd way she was dressed.

The woman wore a navy blue polyester skirt that came down to the tops of her muddy sneakers, a white, long-sleeve blouse, a flowered blue-and-red apron and a man's white handkerchief tied like a head scarf over her thin red braids. The buttons had been cut off her shirt, and the garment was pinned together with what appeared to be safety pins, fastened on the inside.

No wonder Irwin and Hannah's girls were gaping at the Englisher. For an instant, Hannah wondered if this was some sort of joke, but *ne,* she decided, this poor woman wasn't trying to poke fun at the Amish. Maybe she was what the English called a *hippie.* Whatever she was, Hannah felt sorry for her. The expression in her eyes was both frightened and confused, but more than that, she appeared to expect Hannah to be angry with her — perhaps even throw the two of them back out into the storm.

"I'm Hannah Yoder," she said in her best schoolteacher voice. "Did your car break down?"

The Englisher shook her head and lifted the child into her arms. "I . . . I hitched a ride with a milk truck driver. But he let me off at the corner. We walked from there."

"Where were you going?" Johanna asked. "The two of you rode in a milk truck? With someone you didn't know?"

The Englisher nodded. "You can pretty much tell if somebody is scary or not by looking at their eyes."

Johanna met Hannah's questioning gaze. It was clear to Hannah that for once, even

15

wise, sensible Johanna was dumbstruck.

"I'm Hannah," she repeated. "And these are my daughters Johanna —" she indicated each one in turn "— Susanna and Rebecca. This is Irwin." She turned back toward the rocker by the window. "And Aunt Jezzy."

The stranger nodded. "I'm Grace . . . and this is my boy, Dakota."

"Da-kota?" Susanna wrinkled her nose. "That's a funny name."

The young woman shrugged, holding tightly to the child's hand. "I thought it was pretty. He was a pretty baby. I wanted him to have a pretty name."

She had an unfamiliar accent, not one Hannah was familiar with. She spoke English well enough. Hannah didn't think the stranger was born in another country, just another part of America, maybe Kansas or farther west.

"Oh, you must be as cold as the child," Hannah said. "Rebecca, fetch a blanket for our guest."

Grace held out a hand to the warmth of the woodstove. Hannah noticed that her nails were bitten to the quick and none too clean.

"Are you *Plain*?" Hannah asked in an attempt to solve the mystery of the unusual clothes.

The woman blinked in confusion.

"You're not Amish," Hannah said.

"Maybe she's Mennonite," Aunt Jezzy suggested. "She might be one of those Ohio Old Order Mennonites or Shakers. Are you a Shaker?"

"I'm sorry . . . about the apron." Grace brushed at it. "It was the only one I could find. I looked in Goodwill and Salvation Army. You don't find many aprons and the only other one I saw had something . . . something not nice written on it."

Hannah struggled to hide her amusement. The apron was awful. It had seen better days and was as soaked as the rest of her clothes, but the red roosters and the watermelons printed on it were definitely not like any Mennonite clothing Hannah had ever seen.

"Would you like some clothes for your little boy?" Johanna offered. "We could dry his trousers and shirt over the stove."

Grace pressed her lips together and nodded. "That's nice of you."

"And something hot to drink for you?" Johanna suggested. "Tea or coffee?"

"Coffee, please, if you don't mind," Grace answered. "I like it with sugar and milk, if you have milk."

"We have milk." Susanna smiled broadly.

17

"Maybe Dakota would like some hot milk or cocoa," Hannah said, noticing the way the boy was staring at a plate of oatmeal cookies on the counter. "He's welcome to have a cookie with it, if you don't mind."

"He'd like that," Grace stammered, shifting him from one slender hip to the other. "The cocoa and a cookie. We missed dinner . . . being on the road and all."

Hannah thought to herself that Grace had missed more than *one* dinner. The girl was practically a bag of bones. "Let us find you both some dry things," Hannah offered. "I've got a big pot of chicken vegetable soup on the back of the stove. That might help both of you warm up." She smiled. "But I'm afraid you're stuck here until morning. We don't have a phone, and it's too nasty a night to hitch the horses to the buggy. In the morning, we'll help you continue on your way."

"You'd do that? For me?" Grace asked. She sniffed and wiped her nose with the back of her hand. Her eyes were welling up with tears. "You don't know me. That's so good of you. I didn't think . . . People told me the Amish didn't like outsiders."

"*Ya,*" Hannah agreed. "People say a lot about us. Most of it's not true." Then she looked at the stranger more closely. What

18

was there about this skinny girl that looked vaguely familiar? Something . . . Something . . . "What did you say your last name was?" she asked.

Grace shook her head. "I didn't."

Hannah had the oddest feeling that she knew what the stranger was going to say before she said it.

"It's Yoder." The young woman looked up at her with familiar blue eyes. "Same as you. I'm Grace Yoder."

CHAPTER TWO

"I'm Grace Yoder," Grace repeated, gazing around the room expectantly. "And I've come a long way . . . from Nebraska." Standing here in this fairytale kitchen, her clothes dripping on the beautiful wood floor, all these strangers staring at her, Grace was so nervous that she could hardly get the words out. "We went to Pennsylvania where he grew up, but people said he moved here. I hope this is the right house. We're looking for Jonas Yoder." She paused for a long moment. "Please tell him his daughter and grandson are here to see him."

"Was in der welt?" the older woman in the rocking chair, Aunt Jezebel, exclaimed. *"Lecherich!"*

"Ne," the oldest sister said to Grace. Her expression hardened. "You've made a mistake. Jonas Yoder isn't your father. He's ours."

The younger girl, Rebecca, looked at her

mother. She was holding a blanket she'd just fetched. "Tell her, Mam! Tell her that she's wrong! It's a different Jonas Yoder she's looking for. She can't be . . ." She took the hand of her younger sister, the one who looked as if she had Down syndrome, and squeezed it tightly.

"*Absatz,*" Hannah said. "Stop it, all of you." She moved closer to Grace and touched her chin with two fingertips, tilting her face up to the light. She looked into her eyes, and when she spoke again, her voice was kind. "What is your mother's name?"

"Trudie," Grace answered. "Trudie Schrock. She was Trudie from Belleville, Pennsylvania, and she was born one of you — Amish."

"Trudie Schrock?" the older woman said loudly from her chair. "I know that name. Trudie's aunt was a friend of Lavina. Trudie was the third daughter in the family, tenth or eleventh child. The Schrocks had a lot of children."

"And her name was Trudie? You're sure of it, Aunt Jezzy?" Johanna — the one with the attitude — asked.

"*Ya.* For sure, Johanna. That Trudie's the only one who didn't join the church. It hurt her family *haremlich* . . . terrible bad. Her father was a preacher, which made things

21

worse. But there was never any talk of the girl being in the *family way.* Trudie left home and they never heard from her again. Must be some other Jonas this girl's looking for."

Grace didn't know what to say, but she knew she'd come to the right house.

Hannah shook her head. "*Ne,* Aunt Jezzy. Jonas told me, before we married that . . . he and Trudie Schrock . . . that I wasn't his first serious girlfriend."

"But not . . ." Johanna twisted her fingers in the hem of her apron looking from her mother to Grace and back to her mother again. "Dat would never . . . To make a baby with a girl not his wife. He couldn't have . . ."

"Hush," Hannah said. "Don't be a child." She waved toward the table. "Come and sit, Grace. Was your mother certain? That Jonas . . ." She sighed, was quiet for a moment, and then went on. "I should have seen it the moment you walked into my kitchen. You have my Jonas's red hair . . . his blue eyes. And you have the look of your sisters."

Grace swallowed, feeling a little dizzy. This was even harder than she thought it would be. She felt as if she was going to cry and she had no idea why. Her gaze moved from person to person. "I have sisters?"

Hannah nodded. "I'm Jonas's wife, and that makes my daughters — our daughters — your sisters." She waved toward the stunned girls. "These three are your sisters, and there are four more. Ruth, Anna, Miriam and Leah. Leah is in Brazil with her husband, but the other girls live close by."

Grace's knees felt weak. Her stomach felt as if a powerful hand was tightening around it, but at the same time, the feeling of relief was so intense that she thought she might lift off the floor and float to the ceiling. This good woman, this Hannah believed her! They didn't think she was a con artist. Giddy and light-headed, she took the chair that Hannah offered. "Could you tell him I'm here?" she asked again in a breathless voice. "My father?"

"Did your mother send you to find him?" Hannah asked, a little bit like the way the police asked questions. Grace had never been questioned by the police, but her Joe had. Many times.

Grace shook her head. "She died when I was eleven. She never told me anything about her past. A friend of hers, Marg, told me what little bit I know. She and my mother danced . . . *worked* together in Reno. Trudie and me moved around a lot, but she and Marg shared a trailer once

23

when I was little."

"Your mother?" Hannah asked. "You called her Trudie?" Lines of disapproval crinkled at the corners of her brown eyes.

Grace nodded. "Trudie was nineteen when I was born, but she looked younger. She never wanted me to call her Mom. She said we were girlfriends, more like sisters. I think it was so guys — *other people* — wouldn't guess her real age. She was pretty, not like me. She had the most beautiful blond hair and a good figure."

"Verhuddelt." The older woman muttered as she retrieved the ball of yarn that had fallen out of her lap and rolled across the floor. "Such a mother."

"No," Grace protested. "She took good care of me. I never went hungry or anything." *Well, not really hungry,* she thought. Memories of sour milk and stale pizza washed over her, and she banished them to the dark corners in her mind. Trudie had always done her best, and she hadn't run out on her like some other moms. Grace had heard lots of horror stories from the kids she'd met in the Nevada foster homes where the state had stashed her after her mother died. Raising a child alone was hard — Grace had learned that lesson well enough. She wasn't going to let anybody

24

bad-mouth Trudie.

"She did the best she could," Grace said. "She was smart, too, even if she didn't have much education. She could speak German," she added. "When she was mad, she always used to . . ." She trailed off, remembering that the angry shouts had probably not been nice words.

"I'm sorry that your mother passed." Hannah sat down and reached out to Dakota. "Here, let me hold him. Rebecca, could you get that cocoa? And hand that blanket to Grace."

The sister named Susanna offered a big cookie. Dakota shyly accepted it, but bit off a big bite.

"Remember your manners," Grace chided, accepting the blanket and wrapping it around her shoulders. She was so cold, she was shivering. "Don't gobble like a turkey. You'll choke."

Susanna giggled. "Like a turkey," she repeated.

Dakota nestled down in Hannah's lap, almost as if he knew her. His eyelids were heavy. Grace was surprised he'd been able to stay awake so late.

Hannah ran her fingers through Dakota's thick dark hair. "How old is he?"

"Three. He was three in January."

"His father?"

"Dead."

"He's little for three," Aunt Jezzy observed.

"But he's strong. He was always a good baby, and he's hardly ever sick. His father wasn't a big man." Grace looked into Hannah's eyes and tried to keep from trembling. "Could you tell Jonas I'm here? Please. I've come a long way to find him."

"How did you get all the way from Nebraska to Pennsylvania? Do you have a car?" Hannah asked.

Grace sighed. Her father's wife was stalling, but she didn't want to be rude. After all, Hannah had let her into the house and hadn't kicked her out when Grace told her who she was. "We had a car, but the transmission went out on the Pennsylvania Turnpike. It wasn't worth fixing, so we left it." She looked down at the floor. No use in telling them that the insurance had run out two weeks ago and that she had barely enough money for food and gas to get them to Belleville, let alone repair a 1996 Plymouth with a leaking radiator and 191,000 miles on it.

"So you went on to Belleville and then came here looking for Jonas?" Hannah looked thoughtful.

"I'm not asking for money. I don't want anything from him or from any of you. I just want to meet him." Grace chewed on her lower lip. "Since Trudie died, I haven't had any family." She hung her head. "Not really." She looked up again. "So, I thought that if I found my father . . . maybe . . ." Her throat tightened and she could feel a prickling sensation behind her eyelids. Grace took a deep breath. She didn't need to tell her father's wife the whole story. She'd save it for him. She looked right at Hannah. "I need to talk to my father. *Please*," she added firmly.

Hannah clasped a hand over her mouth and made a small sound of distress. "Oh, child." She closed her eyes for a second and hugged Dakota. "Oh, my poor Grace. It pains me to tell you that your father . . . Jonas . . . he died four years ago of a heart attack."

Grace stared at her in disbelief. Thank goodness she was sitting down; her legs felt a little weak. Dead? After she'd come so far to find him? How was that possible? *Bad things come in threes, and if you don't expect much out of life, you won't be disappointed.* Her mother always said that. But the awful words Hannah had just spoken were almost more than she could bear.

27

Her father was dead, too?

Dear God, Grace thought, *how could You let this happen? First my mother, then Joe and now my father.* Now she was glad they hadn't eaten since her breakfast of Tastykakes. If she had anything in her stomach, it would be coming up.

"I'm so sorry," Hannah said. "It must be a terrible shock to you. We've all had time to get used to Jonas's passing. We miss him terribly. He was a good man, your father, the best husband in the world."

"Not so good as we thought, that nephew of mine," Aunt Jezzy observed, more to herself than the others. "Not if he fathered a child and didn't take responsibility for her."

"Hush, now, Aunt Jezzy," Hannah softly chided. "We shouldn't judge him. Jonas was a good man, but he was human, as we all are." She kept her gaze fixed on Dakota's sweet face. "He told me that he and Trudie Schrock had made a mistake, and that he'd repented of what he'd done. She left, suddenly, without telling him. No one knew where she went. She just left a note, telling her father that she didn't want to be *Plain* anymore. Jonas never knew about you," she told Grace, lifting her gaze. "You have my word on it."

Grace nodded, trying to get her bearings again. Trying hard not to cry. What was she going to do now? Her whole plan had been based on getting to her father. She was going to come to him, tell him the mistakes she'd made and beg him to let her into his life. She was going to promise to make only good choices from now on, to find a good man who wouldn't lie to her and deceive her. She was going to tell him she wanted to become —

"So." Hannah smiled at her with tears in her eyes. "What do we do now, you and me? Where do we start, Grace Yoder?"

Grace felt shaky, her mind racing. What *did* she want the Yoders to do with her? What was her plan B? Joe always said you had to have a plan B. "Maybe I could have that cup of coffee?"

Hannah chuckled. "You have your father's good sense, Grace. Of course you shall have your coffee, and the soup I promised. Then we'll all take ourselves off to bed. You'll stay here tonight, and I won't hear any arguments. I'll put you and Dakota in the guest bedroom."

"You'll just let me stay?" Grace asked, truly surprised by Hannah's kindness. Especially after the news Grace had just dumped in her lap about her husband. "You don't know me. I could be a thief or an ax murderer."

Hannah smiled at her. "I doubt that, not if you're Jonas's girl. A straighter, more God-fearing man never lived. He might have stumbled once, but he never faltered. I'm sure you're as trustworthy as any of your sisters."

Susanna giggled. "A sister."

"Thank you," Grace managed. "Thank you all." She looked at the women and the boy, all looking at her.

Exactly what she was going to do now?

Grace hadn't thought she'd be able to sleep a wink, but she'd drifted off to the sound of rain falling against the windowpanes and the soft hum of Dakota's breathing. And when she'd opened her eyes, it was full morning, the rain had stopped and the sun was shining.

My father is dead, she thought. She'd come all this way, only to find out that he was as lost to her as Trudie. She felt numb. What was plan B? Where did she go now? What did she do?

"I'm hungry," Dakota said, interrupting her thoughts. "Can I have more cookies?" He popped his thumb in his mouth.

"No cookies this morning," she said.

No one had said a thing about Dakota's dark skin the night before, but she'd be ready for their questions. When Hannah and her sisters asked, and Grace was sure they would, she'd tell the truth — that Dakota's father had been Native American. Marg had said that the Amish were backward, old-fashioned and set in their ways. Grace hoped that didn't include judging people by the color of their skin, because if they couldn't accept Dakota, then she wanted no part of them.

But they hadn't *seemed* to care.

Grace looked down at Dakota's little face as her mind raced. Plan B. She had to have a plan B. But maybe . . . maybe plan B should be the same as plan A. Or close. Why couldn't it be? Hannah had been so nice to her. So welcoming.

"Cookies aren't for breakfast," she told her son as she got out of bed and put her arms out to him. "But I'm sure Miss Hannah will be able to find something for you in her kitchen."

Just thinking of that kitchen made a lump rise in Grace's throat. It was exactly the kind of kitchen she'd expected to find in her father's house, only better. It was big and warm and homey, all the things that the kitchens she'd known in her life weren't.

31

And the Amish she'd met last night, even suspicious Aunt Jezzy and tough Johanna, were right for Hannah's kitchen.

What would it have been like to grow up here? she wondered. *To belong to a world as safe as this one? To be part of a family who could welcome total strangers into their home and feed them and give them a place to sleep without asking for anything in return?*

It all seemed too much. She'd just do what she'd always done when things got scary or uncertain. She'd do what was most important first and worry about the rest later. And now, finding something to feed her hungry child was what mattered. Plan B could wait.

She tidied the two of them up in the bathroom, took Dakota by the hand and, heart in her throat, led him back to the spacious kitchen.

Grace could smell coffee, bacon and other delicious odors coming from the kitchen as she walked down the hall. "Now, you be a good boy," she whispered to Dakota as she led him by the hand. Nervously, she slicked his cowlick back and tried to pat it down. "Show all these nice people just how sweet you are."

Hannah, two of the sisters that she'd met the night before and Aunt Jezzy were gathered at the kitchen table.

"Miriam's taking my place at the school this morning," Hannah explained. "You'll meet her, Ruth and Anna later. And this . . ." She waved toward a thirtyish brown-haired man in a blue chambray shirt and jeans sitting at the head of the table. "This is our friend John Hartman. John, this is Grace."

Grace nodded. He didn't look Amish to her. His hair was cropped short, almost in a military cut, and he had no beard. Definitely not a cowboy type; he was nice-looking in an old-fashioned, country way.

John rose to his feet, nodded and smiled at her. "Pleased to meet you, Grace."

"He's having breakfast," Susanna explained as John sat down again. "He eats breakfast here a lot. He likes our breakfast." She picked up Dakota and sat him next to her on an old wooden booster seat in a chair.

"I stopped by to check on one of Johanna's ewes that got caught in a fence and Susanna caught me and . . . forced me to the table."

Grace wanted to ask if he was a farmer; it sounded as if he knew something about animals. She liked animals, especially dogs, and she'd always felt more at ease around them than people. The best job she'd ever had was working at a kennel where she cleaned cages and took care of dogs boarded there while their families were on vacation. Trying not to say the wrong thing in front of her new family, though, she decided that the less she said to a strange man, the better.

Susanna laughed. "You're silly, John. You said you were sooo hungry and Mam's biscuits smelled sooo good."

"I did and they do," he agreed.

"He wanted to get married with Miriam," Susanna happily explained, offering Dakota a cup of milk. "But she got married with Charley."

John's face flushed, but he shrugged, and looked right at Grace. "What can I say?" He grinned. "Always a bridesmaid, never a bride."

The others were laughing, so Grace forced a polite smile. John seemed like a stand-up guy, a real gentleman. As she accepted the cup of coffee Hannah handed her, Grace couldn't help wondering why her half sister had turned John down. If a man as good-looking as John, who had a job he could work when it rained, asked her, she'd marry him in a second.

CHAPTER THREE

John finished off two slices of scrapple, two biscuits and a mound of scrambled eggs, but as much as he normally enjoyed Hannah's cooking, he may as well have been eating his uncle's frozen-in-a-box sausage bagels. He couldn't take his eyes off the attractive, almost-model-thin redhead, wearing the strangest *Plain* clothing he'd ever seen on a woman.

Her name was Grace. A pretty name for a pretty girl. He knew he would have remembered her if he'd ever seen her before. She was obviously related to the Yoders; she looked like Hannah's girls. From the attention she was giving the boy, she was probably his mother or at least his aunt. He didn't look like the Yoders, though. And the two of them sure didn't look Amish. So why had they spent the night here?

John was Mennonite, and among his people, staying in the homes of total strangers who shared the same faith was commonplace. Mennonites could travel all over the world and always be certain of a warm welcome from friendly hosts, whether it was for a weekend or a month. But the Amish were a people apart and rarely mingled socially with outsiders, who they called *Englishers.*

" 'Come out from among them and be separate.' " 2 *Corinthians* 6:14. It was a verse that John had heard quoted many times since he'd come to join his uncle's and grandfather's veterinary practice. Because he specialized in large farm animals, many of his clients were Old Order Amish. Mennonites and Amish shared many of the same principles, and because he'd come close to marrying a Yoder daughter, he'd gotten to know the Amish in a way that few *Englishers* did.

Who was this mystery woman with such a haunting look of vulnerability? And what was so important about Grace's visit that Hannah — who *never* missed school — had taken the day off from teaching? John couldn't wait to get one of the Yoders alone and find out.

He lingered as long as he could at the table, having more coffee, eating when he wasn't really hungry and trying his best to engage Grace in conversation. But either she didn't answer or gave only one-word responses to his questions, intriguing him even further.

Eventually, he ran out of excuses to sit at Hannah's table and glanced at his watch. "I hate to leave such good company," he said, "but I have an appointment out at Rob Miller's farm." Repeating his thanks and wishing the others a good day, he gave Grace one last smile, and left the kitchen.

Hannah followed him out onto the porch, carefully closing the door behind her. "Well, what do you think?" she asked, drying her clean hands on her apron. "Of our visitor?"

He wondered whether to play it safe and be polite or to be himself. Himself won. "Um . . . she's nice. Pretty." He met her gaze. "But, Hannah, I'm confused. Grace isn't Amish, is she?"

"*Ne*, John, that she isn't."

"A friend of the family from out of town?"

"None of us had ever laid eyes on her until last night. She came to us out of the storm, soaked to the skin and near to exhaustion. She'd been hitchhiking."

"Pretty dangerous for a young woman," he observed, not sure where the conversation was going.

John could tell that Hannah was pondering something, and that she wanted to talk, yet the Amish tradition of intense privacy remained strong. John waited. Either she would share her concerns or she wouldn't. No amount of nudging would budge her if she wanted to be secretive.

But then Hannah blurted right out, "Grace is my late husband's daughter."

"Jonas's daughter?" John stared at her in disbelief. He'd never heard that Jonas had been married before. "Jonas was married —"

"Jonas and Grace's mother never married. She ran away from the church. Jonas never knew she was in the family way."

John couldn't have been more shocked if a steer had been sitting at Hannah's table this morning. For a moment he didn't know what to say. Jonas Yoder had been one of the most genuinely kind and decent men he had ever known. It just didn't seem to fit that Jonas would . . . "You're certain this isn't a scam of some kind?" He couldn't imagine that the young woman he'd met inside could do anything dishonest, but Uncle Albert had often told him that he was naive when it came to seeing who or what people truly were. "She's not trying to get anything from you? Money or something?"

"She's asked for nothing. She came here

38

looking for Jonas and I had to tell her he'd passed."

Poor Grace, he thought. *How terrible for her. But how terrible for Hannah, too. Not just to hear this news, to learn the awful truth about her beloved husband, but to have to tell his child that he was dead.*

"I . . . believe the girl is who she says she is," Hannah admitted, going on slowly. "Jonas told me . . . confided to me his affection for her mother, Trudie. Jonas was under the impression they were courting, then Trudie left the church and her family and disappeared. Jonas never knew anything about a baby. I would suspect her family didn't, either."

"It's possible, I suppose." John glanced out into the farmyard, feeling so badly for Hannah. Not wanting her to feel uncomfortable. This kind of thing was a delicate matter. Unwed young Amish women occasionally got pregnant, but it didn't happen often. And when it did, there was repentance, then a quick wedding and the matter was settled. "She has the same color hair as your girls."

"And Jonas's blue eyes."

John glanced toward the kitchen door, picturing again the guarded expression in the young woman's gaze. "I thought there

39

was something familiar about her. She favors Johanna, not as tall, and she's a lot thinner, but . . ."

"Too thin by my way of thinking, but Miriam was always slender, too."

John nodded. It hadn't been easy, coming to accept losing Miriam. But after two years, he could see her or hear her name without feeling as though a horse had kicked him in the gut. And he could see that she'd made the right decision. She wouldn't have been happy leaving the Amish, so as much as he hated to admit it, Charley was right for her.

"How do you feel about Grace coming here?" he asked. "It must be a shock to you."

"*Ya,* a shock. It . . . is. My Jonas was as capable of making a mistake as any of us. As much as I loved and respected him . . ." She shrugged. "A bishop, my Jonas was, but I knew him to be a man first. His girls think him perfect." She chuckled. "And the longer he's dead, the more perfect he becomes."

John grinned. "That happens a lot, and not just in your family. My mother and father didn't always see eye to eye, but once he died, Mom promoted him to sainthood."

Hannah laced her fingers together. "Whatever Jonas's faults, he repented of them and asked God's forgiveness every day. When he passed, he left me the means to care for his children and myself and nothing but good memories." She walked down the steps and into the sunshine.

John followed her, giving her a moment before he spoke again. "You are the most remarkable person, Hannah Yoder. Most women would have been furious or so hurt, so bitter that they couldn't have considered inviting the girl into their home."

"Ne." She shook her head and slowly slid down to sit on the top step of the porch. "I am not remarkable, only numb, like after you hit your thumb with a hammer. Before the pain starts."

"But you didn't take it out on Grace. That's what matters. You had compassion for a stranger."

"Why should I blame her? None of this is Grace's fault. She's innocent. I need to remember that. My girls will look to me to see how to treat her, as will the community."

"I'm just saying, as your friend, that you have a right to be upset." He folded his arms over his chest. "Her coming here changes your family. Forever."

"And her," Hannah said. "I don't believe she has had an easy life. Her mother died when she was a child."

"So she's left without a mother or a

father?" *No wonder she had the look of a lost puppy,* he thought. But then, he corrected himself. *Not a puppy, but a feral kitten, wanting so badly to be loved, but ready to scratch to defend itself.* "So now that she's here, what are you going to do with her?"

Hannah frowned ever so gently. "Honestly, John, I have no idea."

Later, after John left and the breakfast dishes were cleared away and Rebecca and Jonah had left for the other sister's house, Grace watched as Johanna settled at the kitchen table with a pile of quilting pieces. Her daughter sat beside her, playing with her own squares of cloth. Just as the night before, Johanna seemed stiff and reserved. Grace couldn't blame her. It wasn't every day a stranger showed up claiming to be a long-lost sister. Katie, however, was all dimples and giggling personality in her Amish dress, apron and white cap.

"How old are you?" Grace asked the child.

"Drei!" Katie held up three fingers.

"My goodness, you're a big girl for three," Grace said. She and Dakota were the same age, but Katie was nearly a head taller and much sturdier. Shyly, her son hid behind her skirt and peered out at Katie. "Come out and meet Katie," she said, taking his hand. She squatted down so that she was closer in size to the two of them. "Katie, this is Dakota."

He stared at her, and Grace ruffled his hair. No matter how much she slicked it down, his coarse Indian hair insisted on sticking up like the straw in a scarecrow. No wonder Joe had grown his long and braided it. "Say hello," she urged her son.

" 'Lo," he managed. Grace could tell that he wanted to play with Katie. Since she'd had to pull him out of day care back in Nebraska, Dakota had missed his friends.

Katie put a finger in her mouth and stared back.

"She doesn't speak English very well yet," Hannah said, walking into the kitchen. "But she understands it. Most children learn when they start school, but Jonas always insisted that we use both English and Pennsylvania Dutch at home, so the girls wouldn't feel uncomfortable among the Englishers." She looked at Johanna. "I know you need to get to your quilt, but if you, Grace and Susanna could hang out the wash, I can get that turkey in the oven." She glanced at Grace. "I hope you don't mind. We all pitch in to do the housework."

"Sure," Grace said. "I'll be glad to help. Tell me what to do."

"I'm just glad we've got sun and a good breeze," Hannah said. "We're expecting company this afternoon, and I've washed all the sheets. If it had kept raining, they would have been a mess to get dry."

"Right," Grace mused. "No electric dryer." Then she considered what Hannah had just said and started to get nervous. About her new plan: plan B. "You're getting company? I guess I picked a bad time to show up here."

"Ne," Hannah said. "It's a big house. Friends of ours, the Roman Bylers, have relatives moving here from Indiana. Sadie and Ebben King bought the little farm down the road from us. They'll be part of our church. Two of their sons and a daughter, all married, live here in Kent County, so they decided it was time to move east. They'll be staying with us until the repairs are done and they get a new roof on."

Grace wanted to ask why the Kings were staying with the Yoders instead of their own relatives, but she thought it better to keep her questions to herself. She didn't want to be rude.

"They have one boy left at home," Hannah continued. "David. He's their youngest. He's like our Susanna. Special."

It took Grace a second to realize what

44

Hannah meant. The son must have Down syndrome like Susanna. She nodded in understanding.

"Get those wet sheets, Johanna?" Hannah asked.

Minutes later, Dakota and Katie were happily playing together under Hannah's watchful eye in the kitchen, while Grace, Susanna and Johanna hung laundry on the clothesline in the backyard.

As Grace hung a wet sheet on the line running between two poles, she took in her surroundings. It seemed almost too good to be true to Grace. The white house, the wide green lawn with carefully tended flower beds, and not a car or TV antenna in sight. The only sounds she heard were the breeze rustling through the tree branches, the creak of the windmill blades and the joyous song of a mockingbird.

Johanna, her mouth full of clothespins, was intent on attaching a row of dresses — blue, lavender and green dresses — while Susanna and Grace hung items from an overflowing basket of towels and sheets. Grace eyed the dresses and aprons wistfully. Today she'd put on a clean blouse from her bag, but she didn't have another long skirt or apron so she'd had to put the same ones on again. Susanna and Johanna both wore modest Amish dresses in different shades of blue with white aprons and stiff white caps. Grace felt foolish with her men's handkerchief tied over her hair, but no one had mentioned it, so maybe it wasn't as bad as she thought.

Susanna hummed as she worked, but her older sister was clearly out of sorts. After a while, Grace took a deep breath and peered over the clothesline at Johanna. "I don't blame you," she said in a low voice.

Silence.

"I can see how it would be upsetting," Grace went on. "Me coming here."

Johanna reached down for a boy's pair of blue trousers. "If you must know, I'm not sure I believe you. I don't want to see my mother hurt."

Grace felt her cheeks burning. She'd expected her stepmother to be the one who would try to deny her, not a sister. Not that Grace had even expected a sister. She'd never allowed herself to think any further than finding her father and hoping he'd claim her. Oh, there had been a family in the background in her daydreams, sort of a shadowy idea of younger brothers, but never in a million years had she considered that she'd find seven sisters.

And Johanna had been a surprise. She and

Johanna looked so much alike, almost like twins, although Grace was shorter and skinnier. It was weird to Grace, seeing a stranger who looked so much like the face she saw in the mirror every time she brushed her teeth. And their light auburn hair, a shade you didn't often see, was exactly the same color that Marg had said that Grace's father's had been.

"Trudie's man was a ginger-haired, blue-eyed Amish hottie," Marg had told her.

Grace was so sorry she'd never get the chance to meet Jonas. It wasn't fair. But when had life ever been fair to her?

"Think what you want about me," Grace said stubbornly to Johanna. "I'm here, and I'm just as much Jonas's daughter as you are."

"Maybe," Johanna said. "That remains to be seen."

"What are you arguing about?" Susanna demanded, pulling the clothesline down so she could see them over a row of towels. "Don't be mean, Johanna."

"I'm not being mean."

"Are, too." Susanna planted her chubby hand on one hip and stuck out her chin. "Mam said be nice to Grace. She's our sister."

"She might be our sister, but she might

not, Susanna Banana. She might be a stranger just *pretending* to be our sister."

Susanna shook her head. "I like her, and I like Dakota."

"But what if she's trying to trick us, just saying she's our sister?" Johanna argued.

"Doesn't matter," Susanna said firmly. "Maybe God wanted her to come here. She needs us." Her head bobbed. "*Ya,* and maybe we need her. It doesn't matter if she's a real sister. She can be one, if we want her to, can't she?"

Grace turned toward Susanna as tears gathered in her eyes. "Thank you," she managed, before dashing across the grass and back into the house. She wanted to go into her room, to fling herself on the bed, shut the door and try to reason this all out. She didn't trust herself to talk to Hannah or anyone else until she'd regained her composure.

"What's wrong?" Hannah asked as Grace came in the back door.

Grace rubbed at her eyes and sniffed. "Nothing. Must be allergic to something."

"*Ya,*" Hannah agreed. "Must be."

"This is hard," Grace admitted, folding her arms over her chest and looking down at the floor. "I didn't think it would be this hard."

"It is going to be hard for all of us. Maybe Johanna most of all." She glanced at the two children who were busily sorting wooden animals in a toy ark in the center of the floor. "Come with me." She motioned, and Grace followed her into what appeared to be a big pantry off the kitchen. "So the children won't hear," she said quietly. "Don't be too quick to judge Johanna. She has a good heart, but she's had a hard time these last few years. She is a widow, too. Did you know?"

Grace shook her head. "No." So Johanna had lost her man, too? It was creepy how much alike they were. "I'm sorry to hear it."

"He was sick . . . in his mind," Hannah explained. "Wilmer took his own life. Johanna couldn't manage their farm on her own, so she came home to live with us. For a long time, things were not good with her and Wilmer, and she finds it hard to trust people."

Grace nodded. "I can understand that."

"The two of you have common ground," Hannah said. "You both have small children that you love. It's a place to start, *ne*?"

"Maybe." Grace sighed. "But why can't she be like Susanna and just accept me for who I am?"

49

Hannah smiled. "We should all be like our Susanna. She is one of God's special people. She was born with a heart overflowing with joy."

"You believe me, don't you? That I'm Jonas's daughter?"

The older woman hesitated only a second. "*Ya,* I do."

"Then . . ." She peered into Hannah's eyes, thinking about plan B. This was it. This was her opportunity to speak up. "Can we stay — at least for a little while? I won't be a burden, I promise. I'll get a job and pay room and board, and I'll pitch in like everyone else." She glanced at her feet, then raised her head, her eyes wet with tears. "But I need to be here."

"You can stay as long as you like."

Grace looked into Hannah's eyes. "I didn't tell you the whole truth last night. About coming here."

The older woman's face didn't change.

"I did come here to find my father. To meet him. But also . . ." She thought of Dakota and the life she'd led, the life she didn't want for her son. That was what gave her the strength to spit it out. "I came to Seven Poplars to tell my father that I want to be Amish. Like him."

Hannah looked away. "Oh my, Grace."

She sighed.

"It's not impossible, is it?" Grace went on. "Especially because my father — and technically Trudie — were Amish?"

Hannah turned back to her and smiled wryly. "It's not so easy. Sometimes Englishers say they want to be like us, but the world calls to them, too loudly."

"I've seen the world," Grace insisted. "It's too loud."

Again Hannah smiled. And this time she patted Grace's arm. "Best you stay awhile and see if this is the life for you before you make big decisions like that. But whatever you choose, you and Dakota will still be family."

"But I've *already* thought about this for a long time." Grace tried not to sound whiny like Dakota sometimes did. Now that she had plan B straight in her head, she wanted to put it into place. "Being Amish feels right."

"First, you live with us and see how you like it. See if it *still* feels right to you once you've walked in our shoes. In time, if you still think this is the life you would choose, we'll talk to the bishop and see what he says. But first, you must learn *gelassenheit,* the ability to submit your will to that of the elders, the church and the community."

"I will! I'll do anything you say, if only you won't turn us away."

Hanna studied Grace closely. "Can you turn your back on the world? Can you give up your automobiles, your television programs, your telephones and live a *Plain* life?"

"I can. I promise you that that's what I want."

Hannah took her hands. "Then we will try, together. And may the Lord help and guide us every step of the way."

CHAPTER FOUR

"Wake up, *Schweschder*," Susanna called, pushing open Grace's bedroom door. "Wait till you see! Mam sent you new clothes. And Plain clothes for Dakota, too."

Grace stifled a groan. Surely it couldn't be time to get up yet. It wasn't even light out. How was Susanna always so happy this early in the morning? Still, Susanna had called her *sister,* and the word glowed warm in Grace's heart. At least *someone* thought she belonged here.

Susanna placed a kerosene lamp carefully on the dresser, and a circle of soft yellow light spread across the room. "Mam says it's time to get up."

"I'm coming," Grace promised. Getting up before dawn was hard. She'd never been a morning person and rarely came fully awake until her second cup of coffee. Groaning, she pushed back the heavy quilt. She was no quitter. She'd do whatever she

53

had to do to prove to Hannah that she was worthy of becoming one of them.

The room was cool and the feather ticks and quilt that covered the bed toasty. Dakota was snuggled beside her, black hair all spiky and one arm wrapped tightly around his stuffed bunny. Intense love for her son washed over Grace. Dakota was what mattered most in the world to her. His welfare was more important than anything else. The past three days hadn't been easy, but the worst had to be behind her if Hannah had sent them Amish clothing. If they dressed like the rest of the family, it had to be easier for them to fit into the household and the community.

Dakota sighed and burrowed deeper under the covers. She'd tucked him into the trundle bed as she had for the past three nights since Irwin had carried it down from the attic. She knew he should be sleeping in his own bed, but every morning, when she awoke, Dakota was in her bed. Back in Nebraska, he'd slept alone, but since she'd uprooted his life, he didn't want to be apart from her, especially at night. And who could blame him? Seven Poplars was a world apart from a trailer park on the wrong side of the tracks. If she was confused, how much more must Dakota be?

"Mam is making blueberry pancakes," Susanna supplied cheerfully. "And today the Kings come. To stay with us." She bounced from one foot to another in excitement. "Do you want me to take Dakota to the potty and brush his teeth?"

"Would you?" Grace leaned down and whispered in her son's ear. "Wake up, sleepyhead."

Dakota sat up, yawned and rubbed his eyes. A lopsided grin spread over his face when he caught sight of Susanna. Sometimes, Grace found Susanna's speech a little hard to understand, but Dakota seemed to have no trouble at all. He'd taken to Susanna, as Joe would have said, "Like a cowboy to hot biscuits."

Thoughts of Joe were bittersweet, and Grace pushed his image away. So many mistakes . . . but then there was Dakota, her precious son.

Susanna held out her chubby arms, and Dakota scrambled out of the bed and bounced into her embrace. "I'll help him get dressed, too." Dakota waved over Susanna's shoulder as she scooped up a small shirt and a pair of blue overalls and went happily off with her.

Grace's pulse quickened as she looked at the neatly folded stack of clothing. Her hands trembled as she reached for the white head covering on top, but when she picked it up, she couldn't help but be a little disappointed. It wasn't a proper *Kapp,* not like the ones Hannah and her daughters wore. It was white cotton, starched and hand-stitched, but more like a Mennonite head covering than Amish. She'd seen Mennonites in the Midwest; they sort of dressed like everyone else, just more modestly.

The long-sleeved calico dress was robin's egg blue with a pattern of tiny white flowers that fell a good three inches below her knees. It wasn't new, but it fit as if it had been made for her. And once she tied the starched white apron over the dress and added the dark stockings and sensible navy blue sneakers, Grace had to admit that it was a great improvement over the outfit she had arrived in. But it definitely wasn't Amish.

"Small steps," she murmured under her breath. "I should be grateful that Hannah didn't toss me out in the rain." Instantly, she felt guilty for her lack of patience. She dropped to her knees beside the bed and offered a fervent prayer of apology and thanks. "I'm still fumbling in the dark, Lord," she whispered. "I came here looking for a father, and instead You showed me the possibility of a whole family. Help me to do what's right for Dakota and me."

Grace knew that she had much to atone for and much to learn. But surely, a merciful God wouldn't give her a glimpse of heaven, only to snatch it all away.

"Grace?"

Grace rose hastily and turned to see Hannah standing in the open doorway.

"I'm sorry," Hannah said. "I didn't mean to disturb your prayers."

Grace felt her cheeks grow warm. How long had Hannah been standing there? Had she heard her prayer? Unconsciously, Grace put a hand to her cap, checking to see if it was securely pinned in place. "You didn't . . . I mean, I was done. I . . ." She hesitated. "I thought . . . These clothes aren't . . ."

"They're Plain," Hannah said. "Not Amish, but not English, either. Halfway, as you are, Grace. Actually, the dress is a gift from your sister Leah's Aunt Joyce, by marriage. She's Mennonite. Leah married into the family."

"Anna told me that Leah and her husband, Daniel, were missionaries in Brazil. I didn't think that was allowed. . . ."

Hannah's features softened. "Our way, the Old Order Amish way, must be chosen freely by each person. I can't deny that I was surprised that Leah chose another path to God, the Mennonite path, but I accept it as part of His plan."

"Oh." Grace couldn't imagine that her sister would want to leave Seven Poplars for Brazil. And to be Amish and give it up . . .

"Leah's husband, Daniel, has an aunt nearby. Joyce and I have become friends. When I saw her at Byler's and mentioned you, she said that a niece had outgrown some dresses that might fit you. Joyce dropped them off yesterday, but they were a little long."

"I always have to hem stuff," Grace said. "I'm short."

"Your father wasn't a tall man." Hannah folded her arms. "I hope you like the cap and apron. Rebecca sewed them for you."

"I do." Grace took a deep breath. "And I appreciate the clothing. But I don't want to be a burden. I'll get a job just as soon as I can and contribute money to the household." She thought as she spoke aloud. "There must be hotels in Dover. I've worked in housekeeping a lot and most places have a big turnover. I'm not sure what I'd do for transportation. Is there a bus —"

"*Ne.*" Hannah shook her head. "Not permitted."

Grace looked at her. "You mean I . . . we aren't allowed to use public transportation? Is there a rule against —"

Hannah's eyes widened. "You cannot work in a hotel. Housekeeping for English is sometimes allowed in private homes, but the bishop must approve it. He would never allow a woman to work in such a place."

"Being a maid is respectable," Grace argued. "We hardly see the guests at all. I wouldn't be alone. Two girls work together to clean the rooms."

"Too worldly. At Spence's Auction you could work, or at Byler's. Even Fifer's Orchard. But not as a hotel maid. We keep apart from the world."

Grace stared at the hardwood floor. "I'm not sure what I can do, then."

Hannah sighed. "I'm sorry, Grace. If times were better, Eli and Roman could use you in the office at the chair shop. But this winter there's barely enough work for the men."

"I know the economy is bad," Grace said in an attempt to remain positive. "But I've worked since I was fourteen. That's why I thought housekeeping —"

"*Ne.* Maybe Johanna would let you help with her quilting. She sells her quilts in English shops."

Grace grimaced. "I can't sew. I'm all thumbs when it comes to replacing a button."

"Maybe her bees. She has nine beehives and collects honey for —"

"I'm allergic to bees." Grace's shoulders slumped. "The last time I was stung, I ended up in the emergency room. I didn't have insurance, and it took me two years to pay off the bill."

"Then we'll have to keep you away from the beehives. We don't have insurance, either." Hannah met Grace's gaze. "We Amish put our trust in God, and if the worst happens, we help each other to pay the expense." She smiled. "Have faith, Grace. He brought you to us, and He won't abandon you now. We'll put our heads together and find a job for you." Her eyes twinkled. "One that Bishop Atlee and even my sister-in-law Martha will approve of."

From the way Hannah's nose wrinkled when she mentioned Martha, Grace had a feeling that Martha might be harder to please than the bishop. "I don't believe I've met her yet, have I?" Since she and Dakota had come to the Yoder farm, there'd been a steady stream of visitors, but she didn't remember anyone named Martha.

"*Ne,* you haven't. Martha, Reuben and

60

their daughter, Dorcas, have gone to Lancaster to a Coblentz wedding. Reuben is a Coblentz." Hannah brushed the wrinkles out of her starched apron. "Now we should eat our breakfast before it gets cold. It will be a busy day, and I don't want to be late for school."

"If you would tell me what you need done before you leave, I can —"

"Johanna knows. And I should be home before the Kings arrive. We don't expect them until supper time. It all depends on what time their driver picked them up this morning. They spent last night with relatives in Ohio and still have a long drive today."

"It's good of you to have them stay with you."

"Roman's house is small, and they have children. Ebben is a second cousin of your father. They could have stayed with their daughter and her husband, but they live over by Black Bottom. Better Ebben be here to see to finishing their house. You'll like Sadie, a sensible woman with a good heart. Full of fun. Always the jokes, Sadie."

Pondering how different Amish life was than what she'd expected, Grace followed Hannah out of the bedroom. She'd thought her father's people would be stern and

61

solemn, sort of like modern-day Pilgrims. Instead, she'd found gentle ways and easy laughter, making her realize just how much she'd missed out on by not being raised as one of them. *If I had,* she thought, *everything would be so different. And I wouldn't have so much to ask forgiveness for. . . .*

When they reached the kitchen, Grace saw Rebecca, Susanna, Irwin, Aunt Jezzy and the children already seated while Johanna carried a steaming platter of pancakes to the table. Susanna was pouring milk for the little ones as Rebecca slid sausage onto Jonah's plate. No one seemed to mind that Katie already had a mouthful of applesauce before silent prayer.

Dakota looked up at Grace and grinned. She stopped short and stared at him. Dakota's handmade blue shirt and overalls were identical to the ones worn by Johanna's Jonah. Grace had been meaning to trim his hair. It grew so fast that it always needed cutting. But now, she saw that the style was just right. Black hair or not, Dakota looked exactly like any other little Amish boy. Fresh hope welled up inside her as she blinked back tears of happiness. She would make a life for them here. She had to. They could never go back to living as they had before.

"Coffee?" Johanna asked as Grace slid

into an empty chair.

"Yes, please, but I can get —"

"I'm up. Mam?"

Hannah nodded, and Johanna returned with the pot.

The odor of fresh coffee assaulted Grace's senses. She knew from every other cup she'd enjoyed in Hannah's kitchen that the brew would be just the way she liked it — hot, and strong enough to dissolve a spoon, as her mother would have said. Johanna took her seat, and Grace bowed her head along with everyone at the table, including the children.

A moment or two later, everyone was digging into breakfast, more interested in the delicious meal than talking. It gave Grace time to compose herself and smile at Johanna. "I'll be glad to help you get ready for your guests," she murmured shyly.

"Willing hands are always welcome. Anna, Ruth and Miriam are coming over once they finish morning chores at home. Between us, we can roast a turkey, prepare enough food for company and get the house shining."

"And me," Susanna reminded. "I can help."

"You're always a good helper," Johanna said. "And you'll do us a big favor if you can keep Jonah, Katie, Dakota and Anna's

Mae out of trouble while we're busy."

Susanna giggled. "We'll make oatmeal *kichlin*. With raisin faces."

"Cookies!" Jonah chimed in. "I like cookies."

"Me, too," Dakota echoed. Katie clapped her hands. As Johanna had said, Katie was just learning English, but it was clear she understood everything being said at the table.

Grace was just accepting the platter of pancakes from Johanna when Irwin's terrier began to bark. Surprised, Grace turned to look toward the door. Surely her sisters wouldn't be here this early in the morning.

Hannah rose, motioning to the others to remain at the table. When a knock came, everyone stopped talking. Hannah removed her scarf and quickly put on her *Kapp*.

"I hope nothing is wrong," Aunt Jezzy said. "The sun isn't up yet."

Hannah opened the door and laughed. "John, you are an early bird. Come in. We're just sitting down to breakfast."

Rebecca cut her eyes at Johanna and stifled a giggle.

"John!" Susanna cried. "It's John."

Everyone was looking at him, but John didn't seem to mind. He stamped his feet and rubbed his hands together. "It's cold out there. You don't have a cup of coffee to spare for a frozen friend, do you?"

"Of course." Hannah chuckled. "Take off your coat and come to the table. We have plenty."

"I was hoping you'd say that," John answered with a grin. "I've been up all night with one of Clarence Miller's cows."

"Bad off?" Johanna asked.

"Delivered safely of twin heifers," John pronounced. "Although it was a near thing. The first one was breech. If Clarence hadn't come for me, I'm afraid they would have lost all three."

"Thanks be to God," Aunt Jezzy said.

John tucked his gloves into his coat pockets and hung his coat on a hook near the door. "I didn't come empty-handed," he said to Hannah. "Clarence just butchered two days ago. He insisted on giving me a ham and a pork loin. I left them in the cold box on the porch. You're welcome to them, and I know you can use them with company coming."

"Grace." Johanna nudged her. "Could you set a plate for John and pour him some coffee?"

Grace nodded. "Sure." John smiled and winked at her as she got up, and she felt herself blushing. What was it about him that made her feel as if she had two left feet? She'd always been more at ease around men than women. But John Hartman was different. When he looked at her, her wits scattered like fall leaves in a windstorm.

"Don't put yourself out for me," he said. "I know where Hannah keeps the cups."

"No," Grace insisted. "You sit. You're company." Thinking about John was distracting, but it made her feel good that Johanna had asked for help. It made Grace feel warm inside to welcome someone into the house. For a few minutes she could almost convince herself that she had always been one of them.

"Look at you," he said, making a show of staring at her. "Dress and apron, prayer cap."

Grace's throat clenched. Was he making fun of her? "Hannah gave them to me," she said. It came out a whisper.

John saw that his teasing had upset her. "I think you look fine," he said with another warm smile. "More than fine. I think you look . . ."

"Plain?" Hannah said, coming to his rescue.

"I was going to say pretty," he answered. "*And* Plain. Nice. The blue brings out the blue in your eyes."

Now everyone was staring at her. Wood-enly, she walked to the stove and reached for the coffeepot.

"Watch it!" John warned, lunging across the room and throwing out a hand to block her arm. "You need a hot mitt. You don't want to burn yourself."

Grace yanked her arm back almost as fast as she would have if she had been burned. For a second, their gazes met, and she saw the real concern in John's eyes. Then she took a step back. "Sorry," she managed. "I didn't think."

"Ne," Susanna said. "You don't want to get a burn. Becca did. Becca burned herself on the stove. She got the blister. Mam had to put medicine on it."

John found a hot mitt and handed it to Grace.

"Thank you," she said. "That was dumb of me."

"Not dumb," he answered in a deep, rich voice. "We all make silly mistakes." He opened a cupboard door, removed a mug and held it out to her. She forced her hands not to tremble as she filled the cup nearly to the brim. "Thank you, Grace Yoder," he said.

Rebecca giggled.

"Come back to the table, you two, before

67

breakfast turns to ice," Hannah called. "You say both calves were heifers, John?"

He gave Grace a warm grin before turning back to the table. "Pretty calves, both of them. Big. A little tired, but they were both on their feet and nursing when I left the barn. Clarence is lucky. They'll make a fine addition to his dairy herd if he decides not to sell them."

"Late in the year for calves," Irwin said between mouthfuls of pancake.

"Or early." John took a chair. "Clarence didn't intend for her to calve in November. He said Reuben's bull broke down the fence between their farms and got into his pasture."

Grace was grateful that the conversation had turned to animals and away from her. She'd heard lots of talk about livestock around the rodeo, and she'd grown used to it. It was clear that John was dedicated to his work. He didn't seem the least put out that he'd had to miss a night's sleep in one of his client's barns. Even on such a cold night.

"I saw your lights as I was on the way home," he was saying. "I hoped that if I threw myself on your mercy, you'd feed me. Yesterday morning, Uncle Albert insisted on making oatmeal from scratch. It was awful, as thick and gummy as paste. He thought it was wonderful, and there was no way I could get away from the table without eating a bowl the size of my head."

Susanna giggled. "The size of my head," she echoed.

"I can't imagine what it would be this morning for breakfast," John continued, glancing across the table at Grace and smiling with his eyes. "I was just hoping it wouldn't be more oatmeal."

"Ya," Irwin agreed. "Probably so."

"That or his French toast," John replied. "And he always burns that. Says charcoal is good for the digestion." Everyone, including Grace and John and the children, laughed at that.

"It must be hard for the three of you," Hannah said. "Three men with no woman to cook for you."

"It's a heavy burden, I can tell you." John grinned again. "I'd do the cooking, but the truth is, mine is worse than Uncle Albert's."

As the meal continued, Grace tried to convince herself that John was just a friend who had stopped by unexpectedly, that she had no reason to think he was paying special attention to her. She tried to eat, but even the coffee seemed to have no taste at all. She forced herself to concentrate on finishing the single pancake she'd put on her plate before John had arrived.

"Another reason for stopping by, besides starvation," John went on. "The young man who cleans our kennels hasn't come in to work for three days. He didn't even call to let us know he had quit. We're desperate for help. I was wondering if Irwin might like to come by after school for a few hours and maybe half a day on Saturdays? What do you think, Irwin?"

"Me?" He looked up. "I don't know, John. Are they big dogs?"

"You like dogs," John said. "Look how good you are with Jeremiah. You'd be cleaning cages, doing some grooming, helping with —"

"Don't know." Irwin stared at his plate and pushed a piece of pancake into a pool of syrup. "I've got chores . . . and homework. Saturdays I'm pretty busy here on the farm."

"Nine dollars an hour to start," John said. "And I could arrange for you to have a ride to the clinic. You wouldn't have to —"

"I could do it," Grace interrupted.

Everyone looked at her.

She took a deep breath. "I used to work in a big kennel. I'm good with dogs. And . . . and I need a job."

John looked surprised. "It's hard work, Grace. Dirty work."

She looked him straight in the eyes. "I'm not afraid of hard work. And I know dogs. I like them and they like me." She glanced at Hannah. Unable to read her face, she looked back at John. "If you'll give me a chance, I promise you won't regret it."

CHAPTER FIVE

"I'd have to talk to Uncle Albert," John said. "But . . . I don't think he cares who is hired, just so he and Sue aren't doing the cleaning. She's our new vet. Dr. Susan Noble. Just joined the practice in the spring. She's the one who helped us get our small-animal business running."

A lump the size of her coffee cup knotted in Grace's throat, but this was too good an opportunity to miss. This was a job she could do. *Please, God,* she prayed silently. *Help me convince them that I'm the right person. If it's Your will,* she added hastily.

She knew all too well that she'd often prayed for things that hadn't come true — from praying that Joe would recover from his terrible accident, all the way to praying that her old Plymouth would make it to her destination. God didn't always answer prayers, but she believed that He had His own good reasons. And it didn't keep her from praying.

"I . . . I'd do a good job. I know I would," Grace heard herself say.

John glanced at Hannah. "Is that something that your bishop would approve of?"

"Cleaning the cages? Is that what you need?" Hannah turned to Irwin. "You're sure it isn't something you'd like to consider?"

Irwin scooped up a forkful of pancake and jammed it in his mouth. "Got homework," he muttered. "Don't like strange dogs."

"*Ya,* we all know how dedicated you are to your education," Hannah said without the hint of a smile. Rebecca twittered and Johanna hid her amusement behind her coffee cup.

Susanna had no qualms about speaking her mind. "*Ne,*" she said. "Irwin hates school. He doesn't do his homework unless Mam makes him."

Irwin washed the last of his breakfast down with milk, mumbled an excuse and fled, grabbing his coat and hat as he went out the door. Jeremiah scrambled after him, hot on his master's heels.

Hannah chuckled. "I think we can safely say that Irwin doesn't want the job, John. Maybe you *should* consider Grace's offer. I see no reason, because she'd be working for you and your grandfather and Albert, that Bishop Atlee should disapprove. Charley's sister Mary still cleans house for you, doesn't she?"

"Yes," John replied.

"You'll give me a chance?" Grace asked eagerly. "I have kennel experience. My foster mother bred all kinds of dogs and sold the puppies. I cleaned cages, fed and groomed dogs, delivered puppies and did basic medical care for five years."

"How many dogs did she have?" John asked.

Grace shrugged. "It depended. Sometimes more than a hundred." She met his gaze. "I suppose it was a puppy mill, but Mrs. Klinger took good care of her dogs. She had a vet that came out to the house regularly. She fed her dogs well, and their cages were always clean and dry." *I should know,* she thought. *I spent enough hours on my hands and knees scrubbing them.*

"Five years." Hannah was watching Grace. Making her self-conscious. "How old were you?"

Grace lowered her gaze to her cup of coffee, then looked up again. "Twelve when I went to live with Mrs. Klinger."

There were three other foster mothers and a group home before Mrs. Klinger, in the year after her mother died. After that, Sunny Acres Kennel didn't seem so bad. Grace had had to work hard seven days a week, but as long as she kept up with her chores, behaved herself in church and didn't fight with the other foster kids, Mrs. Klinger was nice enough to her.

At least she'd gotten to stay in the same school longer than she ever had before. It wasn't like when she lived with Trudie. With her mother, she missed a lot of school. Once, when Grace was eight, she'd gotten off the school bus to find their trailer empty and all their stuff gone. She'd sat on the step crying until long after dark before her mother came back for her.

"It sounds as if you have the experience we need," John said.

Maybe more experience than I care to share or you'd want to hear about, Grace thought as she clasped her hands together under the table where no one would see. Her stomach clenched. She didn't like deceiving good people, but if they knew her for what she really was, they'd show her and Dakota the door.

John nodded. "Let me see what Uncle Albert thinks while Hannah checks with Bishop Atlee."

It was all Grace could do to not let out a

sigh of relief that no one had asked why she'd ended her stint at Sunny Acres at age sixteen. What would they think of her if they knew she'd run away from the foster home? She'd had her reasons, good reasons, but quitting high school and living on her own hadn't been easy. Many a night she'd slept in someone's barn or went to sleep hungry. She'd never stolen anything and she'd never begged. Somehow, with God's help, she'd survived. And she'd never quit going to church wherever and whenever she could. Somehow, sitting in the back of a church, no matter which denomination, had helped to fill the emptiness inside her.

John looked at his watch. "Yikes. I have a surgery this morning. I'd best get back to the clinic." He rose from his chair, taking one last swig of coffee. "Thanks for breakfast. Again."

"And thank you for the ham and the pork loin," Hannah said with a smile. "You're welcome to come to dinner when we cook it."

"I just might take you up on that." He turned his attention to Grace again. "I promise to have an answer for you by Monday. If you're certain you want the job."

Grace nodded. "Definitely. So long as Hannah . . . and the bishop approve." She hoped that working in the same place as John Hartman wouldn't be a mistake. He had a way of making her pulse race and her thoughts scatter every time he smiled at her. It was a pity he wasn't Amish. If he had been . . .

Grace glanced down at her plate and tried to keep from chuckling aloud. If John had been Plain, she'd have made no bones about setting her *Kapp* for him. Because the surest way to make certain her future was secure in this community was to find an Amish husband and tie the knot. If she married into the church and had a home of her own, then no one could ever say she and Dakota didn't belong.

All the way back to the clinic, John thought of Grace and wondered if hiring her would be the right thing to do. He liked her, and that was the problem. If she didn't work out and he had to let her go, it would be awkward, to say the least. But if she did a good job, it would be a relief to know that the cleaning was done properly by someone experienced and reliable.

He wished he knew more about Grace. When Miriam had turned him down for Charley Byler, he'd been badly hurt, so much so that it had been over a year before he'd gone on a single date. Since then, he'd gone out with three different women, two members of his church. He'd enjoyed their company, but none had intrigued him the way Grace Yoder did. There was an air of mystery about her, and he had a feeling that she was someone special.

He chuckled out loud. It had never occurred to him that he might find another potential mate in Hannah's kitchen.

Then he grew serious. What was wrong with him, thinking such things? After he struck out with Miriam, he'd vowed to never become involved with an Amish girl again. And while Grace wasn't Amish yet, it was clear that it was her intention to join the community.

How crazy would it be to risk the same disappointment? Ultimately, Miriam had chosen the Amish Charley over John, a Mennonite. When John had asked Miriam to marry him, he'd offered to convert to her faith if he could continue his veterinary practice. Considering everything, he now felt that would have been a huge mistake and he would have come to regret it. Thank goodness Miriam had realized that, even if he hadn't, at the time.

He'd been born and raised in the Mennonite Church, but he hadn't taken his religion seriously after he'd left his mother's home for college. Like a lot of young adults, he'd been tempted by the world. He was proud to say that he'd never drank alcohol or used illegal substances, but he hadn't always made the best choices. He'd definitely spent too many Sunday mornings sleeping late instead of going to hear God's word.

But after Miriam had married Charley, John had realized how empty his life had become. He'd accepted Uncle Albert's invitation to attend a worship service at Green Spring Mennonite, and he'd only missed Sunday services when veterinary emergencies prevented him from going. He'd started with the regular worship service and then found himself involved in volunteering. He'd put himself through college working as a carpenter, so repairing homes for seniors or helping to build a community hall was rewarding. He'd even participated in a church-sponsored trip to the Ozarks to construct a refuge for abused women.

Returning to his faith hadn't been dramatic or sudden. It had happened slowly, but the strength he gained from knowing that his life was moving in the right direction was vital to his well-being. He'd found peace and purpose. And now, he'd reached a point in his life where he wanted a wife and kids, if God blessed him so.

John hoped he'd make a good husband and a good dad. He'd always liked kids, and he wanted a chance to be the kind of father he'd never had. It had been important for his own father to provide financial support, but it had come at the cost of spending time with his only son. John had always believed that his father loved him, but he'd never been able to bridge the emotional gap between them.

Being a good veterinarian took long hours, but John intended that — if he did have kids — he'd make time to take them fishing, to read bedtime stories and to help with Little League, 4H and, most importantly, to worship with them. He promised himself that he'd remember to show affection and tell his children that he loved them, even if he had to insist on rules they didn't understand.

John hadn't come to those conclusions by himself. What wisdom he had concerning the relationship between a father and his children he'd learned from Uncle Albert, the rock who'd always been there to listen to and guide him.

John knew himself well enough to realize that he was sometimes too quick to form opinions. He'd known Grace Yoder only a few days, and he should have had the sense to be cautious. Yet, he couldn't deny how he felt. The truth was, being in the same room with her made his pulse quicken and his spirits rise. It was too soon to tell if she was as attracted to him as he was to her.

For all he knew, she might have a boyfriend or even be engaged. But he didn't think so. Because she carried the Yoder last name, in spite of having a son, he guessed she was single. If only she didn't have her heart set on becoming Amish . . . When he married, it would for a lifetime, and he didn't want something as important as faith to strain the bonds of his and his wife's union.

He chuckled to himself as he pulled into the clinic parking lot and parked beside his uncle Albert's pickup. He hadn't even asked Grace to go to a movie with him, and already he was picturing her as his wife. He decided to talk to Uncle Albert tonight at supper about hiring her as the new kennel attendant. Grace needed a job, and the practice needed a dependable employee. It would be foolish not to hire her just because he was attracted to her.

If Grace worked at the practice and he saw her every day, it wouldn't take long before he'd find out if there was more to his attraction than her pretty face and cute figure. Instinct told him that Grace was as lonely as he was. From what he could gather, she'd had a difficult life, but didn't feel sorry for herself or want sympathy. It was obvious that she was independent and possessed a keen mind, and she seemed to be an excellent mother. What he had to discover was whether she had a loving heart and a strong belief in God to go with those sparkling eyes.

"Hannah's sure that she's telling the truth?" Uncle Albert said as he removed a family-size aluminum container of lasagna from the oven.

"Are you certain that's been in long enough?" John's grandfather asked. "Last time it was still frozen in the middle."

"I set the timer," Uncle Albert said. "John, would you get those paper plates off the counter? And a roll of paper towels. I forgot napkins again."

"Nothing wrong with paper towels," Gramps insisted. "Works just as well." He poured cranberry juice into three tall glasses. "And get the cheese, will you, John? Parmesan, not the slices of Swiss."

John chuckled. "And I was thinking

Swiss." The few meals the three of them could share were always haphazard. And Gramps had a running joke about the cheese, even though John had been six and visiting for the weekend when he'd removed sliced Swiss from the refrigerator to go with canned spaghetti and meatballs Uncle Albert had heated.

Gramps laughed, folded his newspaper and added it to the stack of magazines and journals that took up a large section of the dining room table. John passed forks around and took his seat. Uncle Albert offered a brief grace before returning to his questioning. "This young woman you're talking about hiring . . . What did you say her name was?"

"Grace," John answered. "Grace Yoder. And I'm sure she's who she says she is. She's one of Jonas's girls, all right. She looks a lot like her sisters — petite, like Miriam."

"And as pretty?" Gramps teased.

John grinned. "Every bit as pretty. But that's not why I think we should hire her. I like her and —"

Gramps groaned. "Here we go again. What's with you and those Yoder girls? Two years ago you were head over heels over Miriam Yoder. And now —"

"Hannah's a fine-looking woman," Uncle

Albert remarked as he scooped out lasagna onto the paper plates. "It's no wonder she has attractive girls."

John hesitated, finding his uncle's comment interesting. If he didn't know better, he'd think Uncle Albert had a thing for Hannah Yoder. "What I was trying to say about Grace Yoder is that she has five years' experience working in a kennel," John said, trying to bring the conversation back around. "We're desperate for help, and Melody is willing to swing by the Yoder farm and pick her up on her way to work."

"It's fine by me." Uncle Albert shrugged. "So long as Hannah won't be upset if the girl doesn't work out. Has the bishop given his say so? You know the Amish, John. They have their ways, and they're set in them."

"Aren't we all?" Gramps asked, and they all chuckled.

"So it's settled." John cut a piece of rubbery lasagna noodle with his fork, trying not to imagine what the Yoders were having for supper tonight. Not supermarket lasagna, that was for certain. "I can offer Grace the position?"

"Of course you can hire her," Uncle Albert said. "We're making you a full partner on the first of the year, aren't we? We trust you, John. If you believe in the young woman, that's good enough for me."

Six o'clock came and went, then seven, too, without word from the King family. Johanna removed the turkey from the oven, wiped her hands on her apron and glanced at Hannah. "Maybe we should go ahead and eat, Mam. The children are hungry."

"I'm hungry, too," Susanna declared from the doorway.

Grace sat down in the rocking chair and pulled Dakota into her lap. It had been a busy day, what with the cleaning and preparing a large dinner for their expected guests. No, she corrected herself, *supper.* The noon meal was what her Amish family referred to as dinner. She'd have to get used to that. "Maybe we could feed the children," she suggested hesitantly. "It won't be long before it will be time to put them to bed."

"No bedtime." Dakota wrinkled his face. "I'm not sleepy."

"A good idea," Hannah declared. "Susanna, if you wouldn't mind eating with the little ones and keeping an eye on them, we can set the small table up here in the corner."

"I can eat with them," Irwin said, abandoning the adult status he usually assumed. "I'm starved."

"Fair enough." Hannah returned to the stove. "If you think you can get those long legs of yours under the table."

"*Ya,*" Susanna agreed with a wide smile. "The little table with the benches."

"Grace," Hannah called. "Would you help Irwin carry the table and benches in from the pantry?"

The next half hour was occupied with the children's meal. The warm kitchen glowed with the soft light of kerosene lamps and the soft voices of Hannah, Rebecca and Aunt Jezzy. Outside, November blackness had settled around the farmhouse, but Grace felt snug and happy. She was content to sit and watch as her son ate and chattered with his cousins. Already, Dakota was using a few Pennsylvania Dutch words. *He fits in,* she thought. *As if he'd always lived here in this safe and loving haven.*

When the children had finished, Grace helped clear away the dishes and silverware before bathing Dakota and leading him, protesting, to bed. She tucked him with his stuffed rabbit, helped him say his prayers and kissed him good-night.

"I like this," he said sleepily. "Can we stay here tomorrow with Jonah and Katie?"

"Yes," she promised. "And the day after that."

"All the time?" Dakota asked. "Can we stay forever and ever?"

"I hope so," she answered. She didn't want to leave Seven Poplars any more than her son did. She knew they couldn't expect to take advantage of Hannah's hospitality forever. Sooner or later, Grace would have to find a permanent home for them.

But first, a job.

"Sing," Dakota urged.

"Hush, little baby,

"Don't say a word," she sang softly as she stroked his head.

"Mama's going to buy you a mockingbird.

"And if that mockingbird don't sing . . ."

Dakota's rhythmic breathing told her that he had dropped off. Taking the lamp, she walked quietly out of the room and closed the door behind her. Her thoughts were still on the possibility of the kennel job at John's veterinary practice. The position seemed heaven-sent, but if she got it, she would have to be careful. She would see John Hartman every day. Regardless of how much she liked him, she'd have to guard herself against him. She'd have to regard him as her boss, nothing more.

Her future and Dakota's lay with some as-yet-unknown Amish man. She would seek out a decent man of the Old Order faith, allow him to court her and marry him. She knew that before the wedding, she'd have to confess her sins, ask forgiveness and be accepted into the church. That would lift a huge burden off her shoulders. It would give her the first real peace she'd felt in a long time. It would be a new life, heartfelt and honest, one in which she could spend the coming years serving God and her community. It was the only way, and John Hartman had no part in it.

CHAPTER SIX

When Grace returned to the kitchen, she found Hannah standing at the back door peering into the darkness. "Have the Kings arrived?" Grace asked.

"No." Hannah closed the door. "It's starting to sleet."

"Early for such bad weather," Aunt Jezzy said.

"Not for Nebraska." Grace stood beside Hannah and looked out. "By now, they're having snow."

"I kept thinking they'd arrive in time for supper," Hannah murmured. She turned to the others. "But there's no reason for us to wait any longer. It could be that they were delayed on the road, maybe spending the night with friends again."

Grace started to ask why they wouldn't call if they were delayed and then remembered that Hannah had no telephone. When she'd asked about it, Anna had told her that there was a phone at the chair shop for emergencies, but once Eli and Roman locked up for the night, a ringing phone would go unanswered. It was against the *Ordnung* to have a landline telephone in a home, and cell phones were looked upon with disapproval by the elders.

"How is Anna?" Hannah asked, changing the subject, perhaps to ease her own concern about the lateness of her guests. She walked to the stove where the prepared meal waited.

To Grace's delight, Anna and her youngest stepdaughter, Mae, had spent the afternoon at the Yoder farm. Next to Susanna, whom she adored, Grace thought she liked Anna best of the sisters she'd met. Anna seemed as open to welcoming her into the family as Susanna. Ruth, the oldest, was pleasant but a little formal, and Grace had spent so little time with Miriam that she didn't really have an impression of her yet. Thankfully, all of them, including wary Johanna, were kind to Dakota.

"Gut . . . gut." Aunt Jezzy began to talk about how happy Anna had looked and how pink her cheeks had been. "She and Samuel are right for each other," the woman said as she removed her knitting needles from her worn canvas bag and began to work on her project. The wool was white and soft as a

kitten's fur. Grace hadn't been able to guess what she was knitting, and she hadn't wanted to appear nosy by asking too many questions, although a hundred buzzed in her head.

"I'm glad," Hannah said as she began to slice the turkey. "Becca, could you mash those potatoes?"

"I'll do it," Grace offered. It was obvious that her cooking skills were hardly better than Susanna's, but she could mash potatoes with the best of them, especially because there were mounds of newly made butter and fresh milk to stir in. They'd boiled a giant kettle of potatoes and kept them warm on the back of the stove.

"*Ya,*" Hannah agreed, but suggested that Grace first dip out just enough for the six of them. "We'll leave the others unmashed, and one of you can make potato salad tomorrow. You can drain them and put the pot in the cold box on the porch for the night."

Rebecca dished up one bowl of green beans and another of creamed corn while Susanna carried applesauce, bread and butter to the table. Again Grace marveled at how smoothly the work went with so many hands to help. It was almost like a dance, with everyone knowing their places and what to do — everyone but her. There were smiles, jokes and laughter bouncing around the cozy kitchen. It might be sleeting and nasty outside, but here, in Hannah's house, was a sanctuary from the world.

"How's the blanket coming?" Johanna asked their aunt as they all gathered around the table.

"It goes quickly." Aunt Jezzy smiled. "It should, as many as I've made of this pattern."

"She's over the morning sickness?" Hannah asked. "I know it troubled her some." She glanced at Grace. "God willing, our Anna will be blessed with a baby in late April or May."

"May Ruth and Eli soon find the same happiness," Aunt Jezzy said, pushing her knitting bag onto a counter. "She's almost as excited about this coming baby as Anna is. She's already sewn a half dozen gowns and undershirts for the little one."

"Ruth was married two years ago," Johanna explained. "She wants little ones badly, but so far nothing. Neither she nor Miriam have gotten pregnant yet. It must be hard for Ruth and Miriam because Leah and Anna were married after them. Leah already has a baby and now Anna has one on the way."

"It took your father and me a while," Hannah said, "but after Ruth, there was no trouble. I have no doubt that you girls will fill this house with grandchildren. All in God's time."

Susanna giggled and put a finger to her lips. "Don't tell Anna's got a baby in her belly," she whispered to Grace.

"A secret?" Grace glanced at Hannah, unsure what to say. Anna and Samuel already had five children, from his first marriage. Anna was younger than she was, and Grace couldn't imagine being the mother of six.

She supposed that she would have to become accustomed to the idea if she wanted to marry again. Most Amish families were large ones, and it would be good for Dakota to have brothers and sisters. She loved children, but considering how difficult it was to be a good mother to one little boy, six young children seemed overwhelming. *So much to learn,* she thought.

Johanna glanced at her with a pleasant expression. "What Susanna means is that we don't talk about it to people outside the family."

But they didn't hide it from me, Grace thought. *Is Johanna starting to like me?* More than anything, she wanted to break through to Johanna. She had the feeling that once Johanna accepted her, the other sisters and the rest of the community would follow.

"And say nothing to the men," Rebecca put in. "Especially not to Samuel. They all know, of course. Men gossip worse than women." She twittered. "But we all pretend not to know about Anna's blessing."

"In this house, between us, we talk, but say nothing to Anna unless she does first," Johanna advised with a serious look. "Some people worry that it's bad luck to say too much about a baby before it arrives."

"But each one is welcome." Hannah motioned for silence for grace. "And each child a blessing to the parents, the family and the church."

They had finished the delicious meal and were clearing away the last of the dishes when Grace heard a horn and the sound of a vehicle pulling into the yard. "Is that the Kings?" she asked.

Rebecca went to the window. "*Ne,* it's a truck. The Kings hired a van."

Johanna opened the door and went out onto the porch. "It's John Hartman," she called. Rebecca grabbed two coats off the rack and hurried after her older sister.

Susanna was halfway across the kitchen

when Hannah waved her back. "*Ne,* it's cold out there." She shook her head. "You stay inside. I don't want you catching a chill. We'll find out soon enough . . ."

"It *is* the Kings, Mam," Rebecca shouted back. "They've come with John."

Grace couldn't help but feel a rush of excitement. Why was John here again? She knew it was too soon for him to tell her if he could hire her or not, but the thought of seeing him made her a little breathless. *It's just the promise of a job,* she told herself. *If I'm lucky, he'll be my boss. Nothing more.* Her life was finally falling into place, and no hunky guy with an easy smile and a twinkle in his eye was going to prevent her from doing what was best for her and Dakota.

Not two minutes later, John, along with an unfamiliar Amish man and woman, and a young man, were stamping onto the porch. Sleet covered the woman's cape and bonnet and the men's hats and coats. All of them were smiling and talking at once as introductions flew and coats were hung up and coffee poured for the guests, all but the son, the one Grace had heard Aunt Jezzy mention as David.

Grace tried not to stare at him, not because he was odd in appearance or because he obviously had been born with the same

challenges as Susanna. It wasn't his short
stature, bowed legs or chubby body that
held her attention. What was so unusual was
that when David pulled off his snowy black
hat, he was wearing a fast-food chain's
cardboard crown under it. Beneath the
crown curled an unwieldy thatch of yellow-
blond hair. David had sparkling blue eyes,
bright as cornflowers, a dough ball of a
freckled nose, a wide mouth and round, rosy
cheeks. He reminded her of a carved
wooden boy she'd once seen on a Swiss
cuckoo clock in a department store window.

David gave Grace a sweet smile and then
turned his full attention to Susanna. His
smile became a wide grin and he stared
unabashedly at Susanna, who had become
pink-cheeked and giggly. "Hi!" he said in a
husky voice. "I'm King David."

Susanna beamed. "I'm Susanna Yoder."

"Hi, Su-san-na." He bounced from one
high-topped shoe to the other. "Hi."

"Hi."

"I'm King David," he repeated.

"You look like me," Susanna said. "Mam,
he looks like me." And then to David she
said, "Will you be my friend?"

"*Ya.*"

"David, remember your manners," his
mother said softly. Sadie King was a stocky

little woman with eyes that Grace decided had once been the exact color of her son's. Love and kindness radiated from them as she spoke. "Your name is David King."

David nodded vigorously. "King David."

His mother chuckled. "Pay no heed to our David. It's his way. He loves that paper hat."

"However did you end up in John's truck?" Hannah asked.

"Van broke down." Ebben King wrapped his hands around a warm mug of coffee. "On Route 13. South of Wilmington. Bear?"

"The van had to be towed to a garage," Sadie explained. "We couldn't think of a way to let you know."

"Our van driver wanted to stay in a motel across from the garage," Ebben added, "but we didn't care to do that. David likes his routine." He trailed off with a shrug. Ebben was tall and slim with graying hair and beard and round wire glasses.

"The tow truck driver, Jay, goes to our church," John explained. "He would have brought the Kings himself, but he was on duty all night. Lots of need for tow trucks in this weather. He knew that I had a lot of Amish clients, and he thought I might be willing to give the Kings a ride to their destination."

"Is *gut,*" Ebben said. "So kind of you to

97

go out of your way on such a night."

John's dark eyes twinkled. "Glad to help out. I would have spent the evening ordering supplies, anyway. By the time I get home, Uncle Albert will have it done."

"Once again you prove what a good friend you are," Jezzy said. "Come now, sit down and eat. You must all be starved."

"Not me," John said. "I'll just —"

Hannah gave him a look. "John Hartman, you can eat a little. So much the girls cooked, and the turkey is still warm."

John, through a willingness to be amiable or because he was really hungry, allowed himself to be ushered to the table along with the Kings. And this time, once Grace had helped to serve up the food family-style, she found herself sitting beside John. Not that she could eat another bite after the earlier meal, but it wouldn't have been polite not to join the others at the long table.

The Yoders and Kings obviously had news of friends and family to share, but they spoke in English out of kindness to her and John and made an effort to include them both in the general conversation. Susanna was unusually quiet, but whenever Grace glanced her way, she saw her youngest sister staring at David. And if he looked at her, she hid her face in her hands and giggled.

"I think Susanna's made a new friend," John said quietly to Grace.

She nodded. "I think so, too."

John laid down his fork and leaned closer. "I talked to my grandfather and my uncle. If you get the okay from your bishop, we'd like you to start at the clinic as soon as possible."

"Really?" She looked up at him. "That's wonderful!" In her excitement, she must have spoken louder than she intended because Aunt Jezzy looked at her in surprise. "Sorry," Grace said, lowering her gaze. "John says that I can have the job. If it's all right," she added.

"I'm sure Bishop Atlee will agree," Hannah said. "He'll be here Saturday for apple pressing. I'll ask him first thing." She smiled. "You remind me, Grace, if I forget. It will be a busy day, a lot of neighbors coming."

"Am I still welcome to bring our apples down?" John asked. "Uncle Albert is still talking about the fun he had last year. I think we've got about ten baskets in the cold storage. Granny Smiths and Arkansas Black."

"Of course." Hannah passed the potatoes to Ebben for a second helping. "And bring your empty gallon jugs. Our cidering gets

99

bigger every year. Last November we had more than a hundred here." She glanced at Sadie. "If the weather is good, we'll have the men set up the tables outside and eat in the yard."

"It will have to get a lot warmer than this." Ebben looked toward the back door. "Have you seen the sleet coming down outside?"

Aunt Jezzy laughed. "You aren't used to Delaware yet. The saying is, *if you don't like the weather, wait an hour. It will change.* It's always a surprise to me, I can tell you, me coming from Ohio."

"Easier winters here than in Indiana." Ebben returned his attention to his plate. "According to my sons."

"They'll be here with their families Saturday," Hannah said. "And your daughter. They all promised to come early and stay late."

"I can't wait to see them," Sadie replied. "We don't have any means to visit anyone until Ebben can buy a new buggy and a driving horse. We had to sell our buggy when we held the farm auction. And the livestock. Too expensive to ship them east."

"It must have been hard to part with your animals," Hannah said.

"*Ya,*" Ebben agreed. "It was, but this place is much smaller than our old farm. I'm not a young man anymore."

"If you're looking for a dependable driving horse, you should talk to my brother-in-law Charley," Johanna suggested. "He deals in livestock, and I know he has at least two suitable horses for sale."

"And a cow," Sadie put in. "I make my own butter and our David likes his milk." She smiled at David. "Are you certain you can eat more turkey?" Her son nodded and kept chewing.

"So you'll be here Saturday?" Grace asked John.

"Try and keep me away. I'd come for the apple pies if nothing else."

"I've never been to a cidering," Grace confessed. "I'm sure Dakota will like it."

"I know he will," John agreed. The others continued to talk about cows and horses, but his attention remained on her. "More children to play with than he can count. How is he doing? Is he settling in?"

"Yes, he is. It's kind of you to ask. And kind of you to offer me the job," she added, "considering that you're taking my word on it that I've had experience."

"I'm sure you'll do fine," John said, helping himself to a serving of chowchow and more coleslaw. He grinned and dabbed at the corner of his mouth with a snowy-white cloth napkin. "It's hard to find good help, and if we suit each other, you'll be doing our practice a big favor."

But will I be doing myself a favor? Grace wondered. John was a nice guy, a sweet guy, from all appearances. He'd done or said nothing that would cause her to believe his interest in her was anything but professional. But that didn't keep the oxygen from draining out of the room when he walked into it, and it didn't help a bit that when she dreamed of an Amish husband later that night, he was wearing John's face behind a neatly trimmed brown beard.

As Aunt Jezzy had promised, the weather did change. By Saturday, the temperature had risen to the sixties and the sun had dried up the soggy yard and fields. By eight o'clock in the morning, a stream of buggies was rolling up Hannah's lane. Grace had never seen so many Amish gathered in one place at one time.

"More than last year," Anna said as she supervised a pair of blond-haired boys unloading endless pies and baskets of delicious-smelling baked goods from her family buggy. "Careful with that bowl of macaroni salad, Rudy," she called to one of them. "We don't want it spilled on the ground for the chickens." She waved. "Naomi!"

A tall girl, about ten or eleven, wearing glasses, helped two younger girls out of the buggy. "*Ya,* Mam. I'll watch they don't get under the horses' hooves."

"Take them into the house, *Schippli.* The big girls are minding the children this morning. You find your friends and have a good time."

"What did you call her?" Grace asked. "I thought her name was Naomi."

Anna chuckled merrily. "She is my *lamb,* my sweet Naomi. Always she helps without me asking. The twins . . ." She shook her head and laughed again. "Full of themselves, Peter and Rudy, but good boys. Not a lazy bone in their bodies. See how they help *Grossmama* down from the buggy. They'll make fine men. *Grossmama,* come. Meet our Grace." Anna leaned close and whispered. "Don't let her upset you. She has a sharp tongue, but she'll make your son gingerbread cookies and spoil him endlessly."

"Grace!" Hannah called from the back porch. "We need you."

"Pleased to meet you," Grace said to the elderly woman, then dashed off gratefully to help in the kitchen. From what she could gather from Rebecca, and remarks Miriam had made to Ruth, their grandmother had been a difficult person *before* old age had begun to cloud her reason. Grace hoped for a good relationship with her, but she was afraid that *Grossmama's* reaction to her son's illegitimate daughter would be less than positive. Grace didn't know if she was ready to confront the matriarch today.

Because so many in the community would be gathered at the Yoder farm for the cider making, she hoped she'd meet some of the eligible Amish bachelors. Aunt Jezzy had hinted as much, explaining that there were nine church districts in the area, and Rebecca or Grace might meet someone they liked. Grace wished she was dressed like her sister in a neat blue dress and white apron and *Kapp,* but she felt pretty in the green calico dress that Hannah had hemmed just in time for Saturday's celebration. If she didn't look exactly Amish, Grace thought that she looked properly Plain, and she'd taken care to get her smaller cap pinned on so tightly there'd be no chance of it coming loose during the busy day.

She hoped that it wasn't the wrong thing to do, actively searching for a husband, but if she didn't make an effort, how could she expect someone to court her? *Court her.* A shiver of excitement made her chuckle. It sounded so old-fashioned, so wholesome. She and Joe hadn't had much of a court-ship. He'd stopped and picked her up along a lonely road where she'd been hitchhiking. It had been an unconventional relationship from the first night she'd laid eyes on Joe, and it never got much better. But that was all in the past. God willing, things would be different here in Seven Poplars, and she'd get a chance to live her life in a better way.

"Grace!" Rebecca poked her head around the door. "Hurry! It's Bishop Atlee. He's in the front room and he wants to see you."

Grace opened the door a little wider. "Did your mother ask him?"

Rebecca grimaced and threw her hands up to signify that she had no idea. "But he wants to talk to you. And he looks —"

"As though he's going to agree?" Grace suggested with more optimism than she felt. Her heart plunged. If she hadn't been prepared to face her grandmother, she was twice as unready to meet the bishop.

"Serious," Rebecca finished. And then as Grace hurried through the kitchen, crowded with busy women, her sister called after her, "Good luck."

CHAPTER SEVEN

Grace clasped her hands together to keep them from trembling as she stepped through the wide doorway into the Yoders' parlor. She'd never been inside, other than to dust the table, fireplace mantel or window seat, but she knew this room was used only for company or important events. As she prepared to face Bishop Atlee, her mouth went dry, her heart raced. She wanted to be respectful, but knowing that her plans for finding meaningful work — indeed, her very future among the Amish — depended on Bishop Atlee's decision made her determined to emphatically state her case. She would not take no for an answer.

She stopped just inside the entrance. Standing at a window, gazing into the side yard, his back to her, was a short, stocky man in black shoes, black trousers and a long black coat with a split tail. Grace took a deep breath and waited. When seconds dragged by without him noticing her, she cleared her throat.

The man turned to face her, a wide-brimmed, black felt hat in one hand. "Grace, it's good to meet you." He tilted his head and smiled sheepishly. "Forgive me. Have you been standing there long? My wife says I'm getting hard of hearing, but I think I just concentrate so hard I forget to listen. I was going over tomorrow's sermon in my head." His cheeks dimpled as he studied her with warm blue eyes.

Grace swallowed, unsure what to say.

He studied her. "*Ya, ya,* you do have the look of your sisters." He stroked a flowing white beard that made him look like an Amish Santa Claus.

Not that the Amish believe in Santa, Grace thought, glad that he couldn't read her thoughts.

He chuckled. "Jonas's girl, for certain." Spreading open his hands in a gesture of welcome, he said, "Child, we are happy to have you in Seven Poplars."

Relief made her insides somersault. She'd expected a tall, stern cleric, not a jolly grandfatherly type. Was it possible that this man was the senior church elder? Or had she made another of her many mistakes? "Bishop Atlee?" she stammered.

"Ya. Ya." His vest-covered belly quivered with amusement. "What were you expecting? You're white as new lard. Did you think I would reject you for your parents' sin?"

"I . . . I didn't know. I thought . . . Old Order Amish . . . all the rules," she managed, before she ran out of breath.

"We are all human, Grace, none more so than me. Every day, we try to follow God's word, but from time to time we stumble." He rocked his head sideways, one direction, then the other. "Then we must ask forgiveness and do our best to live as He instructs us. That's all any of us can do. It would be a hard heart indeed who could turn away a child for being born."

A wave of relief washed over her. "So, it's all right if I take the job?" She struggled to find words. "With the animals . . . at the clinic?"

He shrugged. "Fine by me. Work is always good. Like prayer, for building character. But why are you asking my permission?"

"Hannah said . . . I thought I had to."

"Ah." The blue eyes narrowed, his expression became serious. "I can see that you don't understand what a bishop does in our church," he explained gently. "I'm an ordinary man, chosen by God to serve our community. I do rule on our members' behavior, because it's my duty to give judgment as best I understand His plan for us. But you aren't one of us, Grace. You would have to be a baptized member of our faith for me to instruct you. You must do as you see fit."

"But that's just it," she said. "I *want* to be one of you. I want to be Amish, like my parents were, to live like you do, to worship and serve God as you do."

He sighed and folded his arms over his broad chest. "So Hannah has told me, child. And I wish you well. We all do. We would like nothing better than to welcome Jonas's girl to our fold, but it is hard. Harder to give up the world than you can imagine. I've seen others try, but never have I known a woman or a man to succeed. The pull of the outside life is too strong."

"But I can try? You won't forbid it?"

"Forbid it?" His eyes widened. "I will pray for you, Grace. We will all pray for you, but . . ." He shrugged. "I fear your row will be long, rocky and thick with weeds. Try your best and come and talk to me again in . . . a year, maybe two. Then we'll see."

"But . . ."

"Two years would be better." Bishop Atlee settled his hat over a gray-streaked head of thinning hair. "Now, I must get myself to the barn or my friends will think I'm hiding in the house, trying to avoid the work of sorting apples."

A year? Maybe two? Grace watched as the man made his way out of the parlor and down the hall. "Two years," she murmured, half under her breath. She didn't have that long. How could she stand the wait? In a year, maybe less, she'd hoped to be one of them, to have a husband and a home of her own.

She was sure that the bishop meant well, but he didn't know how determined she could be or how many obstacles she'd already overcome. And most of all, he had no idea why she needed this life for herself so badly . . . why this was the only way. She would show him. She would show them all. She wouldn't fail in this — she couldn't.

"Grace?" Anna's voice penetrated Grace's musing as she appeared in the doorway. "We need your help."

As Grace allowed herself to be pulled back into the noisy hubbub of the kitchen and the preparation of food, she pushed the bishop's warning to the back of her mind. She wouldn't allow his cautiousness to take away any of her excitement and joy over being allowed to take the job . . . or of the cidering.

She had a plan today. Grace loved a plan.

Between working with the other women and keeping an eye on Dakota, she would scout the territory for a new father for him and a husband for her. She hoped he'd be a farmer. It would be good for Dakota to live surrounded by animals and growing things.

And trees . . . she thought wistfully. She hoped that there would be trees around her new home. Trees were solid. They sank their roots deep into the earth and endured . . . exactly what she wanted to do.

In the barn, John and his uncle had easily found a place in the cider-making process where they could be useful. Uncle Albert washed apples, while John carried baskets of them to dump onto the hand-crank conveyer belt. The apples dropped into a crusher before moving on to the press. Fresh, sweet juice poured in streams out of the press into a vat and finally into clean gallon jugs.

Around him Amish men and boys laughed and talked, sharing jokes half in English and half in Pennsylvania Dutch, sometimes interjecting German words into an English sentence and vice versa. Not everyone taking part in today's cidering was Amish; a few outsiders had come to share in the work and camaraderie. Uncle Albert knew most of them, either as clients, friends or both, and John watched as he exchanged good-natured ribs with them. A person didn't spend thirty years in a small county without getting to know nearly everyone.

They couldn't have asked for a better day. The sun was out; the air was crisp and cool without being raw, and there wasn't a hint of a breeze. Best of all, the Yoder barn, clean and neat as always, smelled of hay, apples and healthy animals. It was John's idea of what heaven must smell like. He'd been working for the better part of an hour when Bishop Atlee joined them. The bishop greeted Uncle Albert with a grin and a handshake before pulling off his black church coat and hanging it on a nail.

"Let me take over here, John," the older man offered, when he'd been welcomed by the others. "It will do me good to do a little physical work before we sit down to the noon meal. It's quite a spread those women are fixing, I can tell you."

John wanted to ask him if he'd given permission for Grace to come to work at the clinic, but this wasn't the time or place. Over the past few days, it had somehow become important to John that Grace join the practice, and he didn't want to spoil the day if the church elder had given the wrong answer.

John hadn't caught sight of Grace yet, but he had picked out small Dakota, riding in a child's wagon pulled by an older boy. In his straw hat, denim coat and trousers, he looked exactly like every other Amish boy, although his complexion was somewhat darker than the fair German/Swiss faces surrounding him. He couldn't help wondering about Dakota's father, and if he was honest with himself, hoping that the man was out of Grace's life.

John stepped back and handed the bishop an empty bucket, nearly colliding with Rebecca Yoder, who barely managed to avoid spilling the mugs of coffee she carried. "Sorry," John said. He looked around, hoping to see Grace, but was disappointed. There was a girl in a lavender dress with Rebecca, one of her cousins, but John couldn't remember her name.

Rebecca laughed and dodged around him to hand a cup of coffee to his uncle Albert. She offered the second to Bishop Atlee, but he shook his head. Roland Byler accepted it with a nod, and Rebecca smiled warmly up at him. Roland was a brother to Charley Byler, who'd married Rebecca's older sister Miriam.

John had been treating one of Roland's milk cows for mastitis. He didn't know Roland well, but what he'd seen of him, he liked. Roland was a widower with a son close in age to Grace's Dakota. The Amish didn't usually remain single long after the loss of a husband or wife. Roland was a good-looking man, well-spoken and a hard worker. He had a nice little farm. John wondered if there might be something brewing between him and Rebecca. She was young, but not too young to consider marriage to someone as well-regarded in the Amish community as Roland.

One of the young men from Rose Valley called out to Rebecca's companion. "Dorcas! I like coffee. Didn't you bring me a cup?"

Dorcas giggled and held out the mug to John. He shook his head and thanked her.

His uncle Albert used a long-handled wooden paddle to stir the floating apples in the wash tank, and then glanced back over his shoulder at John. "Can you check if we've had a call from the office? I want to make certain that Bernese puppy is still stable."

John nodded. His uncle had performed emergency surgery the night before on the sixteen-week-old puppy that had swallowed a bottle cap. Normally, John would carry his cell phone with him, but he'd just replaced one that he'd accidently dropped into a horse's watering trough. Considering the process involved in making cider, he'd decided to leave his new one in his glove compartment for safety's sake. He crossed the farmyard to his pickup and had just opened the passenger's door when he heard a child shriek.

By the time John pushed through the circle of children crowded around the swing under the big oak tree, Dakota was sitting up on the ground and screaming at the top of his lungs. Susanna knelt beside him, crying, blood on her hands. "What happened?" John squatted down by the injured child. Whatever had happened couldn't be too serious, he decided. No one who could scream that loud could be critical.

Susanna sobbed and mumbled something, but John couldn't understand.

"What happened?" John repeated. He'd located the site of the injury, a cut on a swelling lump on the back of Dakota's head.

Most of the kids stared wide-eyed as John gathered the hysterical child into his arms, but Johanna's son Jonah spoke up. "Swing," he said. "Caleb fell off," he said carefully in English. "The swing hit Kota."

Susanna rubbed her hands on the grass, threw her apron over her head and cried louder.

"Shh, shh," John soothed. "You'll be all right." Dakota clung to John's neck and buried his face in his shirt. The bleeding had already slowed, and John put pressure on the wound with a handkerchief. Dakota howled again. John started toward the house. He hadn't gone more than a dozen steps when Grace came running toward him.

"How bad is he hurt? Lori Ann said . . ." She broke off as John explained what had happened.

"It looks worse than it is," he said. "Just a bump and a scalp wound. The laceration isn't deep."

Grace put out her arms to take him, but John shook his head. "Let me. We'll take him inside, wash him up and —"

"I can do it," Grace insisted, patting Dakota's back. "It's all right, sweetie, Mommy's here."

"If you want." Reluctantly, John handed over the boy. "If you need bandages, I have some in the truck. I'd really like to examine him, once you've washed it. I can tell you if he needs to go to the emergency room."

"You think he'll need stitches?"

"If he does, I'll drive you to the hospital. Do you have a pediatrician?"

"No, we haven't had time to find one."

"We have a good medical staff at the hospital, and there'll be one on call."

Women had poured out of the house and were offering advice, mostly in Dutch. Hannah arrived, took one look at the two of them, another at the shrieking Susanna and cleared a path. "Take him into the bathroom," she suggested.

"Is Susanna hurt?" John asked. The King boy had found his way to Susanna and was standing by the tree staring down at her. Oddly, he was crying, too.

Hannah went to her daughter, spoke to her and helped her to her feet. "She's fine," she pronounced. "Just scared of blood and afraid that it's her fault Dakota got hurt."

"He'll be fine," John reassured Susanna, smiling.

By the time they got inside, the bleeding had stopped, and Dakota's sobbing had faded to a faint sniffle. Once they washed the back of the boy's head, he could see that the cut was a small one and the bump didn't seem to be getting any larger. "Put a cold compress on it," he advised Grace.

"Do you think he should see a doctor?" she asked.

"Watch him for any unusual sleepiness, dizziness or nausea. I'd say the swing barely grazed him. Head wounds bleed a lot."

"I think I'd feel better if a pediatrician took a look."

"All right. I'll drive you to the hospital."

"It's kind of you, Mr. Hartman."

"John." He smiled at her. "The Amish don't favor titles. Everyone goes by his or her given name. Even children call adults by their first name. You'll have to get used to that."

"There are a lot of things I have to learn about this life," she said, cuddling Dakota against her. She offered him a grateful smile. "I can come to work for you, cleaning the kennels, if the job's still open. Bishop Atlee said it was all right."

"Great." John grinned. "Now, let's get this boy checked out before we miss out on the wonderful dinner you ladies prepared."

Fortunately, the emergency room was nearly empty, and they were in and out of the hospital in less than two hours. John had been right. A little antibiotic ointment, a couple of butterfly bandages and a super-hero sticker completed the treatment. By the time they got back to the Yoder farm, the men were just gathering for the first seating for the meal. Dakota scrambled out of the truck and ran to join Jonah and his new friends as Grace turned to John.

"I can't thank you enough," she said. "For taking us to see the doctor, for offering to hire me, for everything."

"No problem," he said, stuffing his hands into his jeans pockets.

"I want you to know how much I appreciate it. You're a very nice man, John, and I hope we can be friends." She hesitated. "As . . . as well as employer and employee," she stammered. "I didn't mean . . ."

John's smile widened and his eyes lit up. "I know it's not politically correct to say so, but I like you. I like you a lot, and I hope we can get to know each other a lot better. I mean this in the most respectful way. I think you're an admirable woman and a great mother. Would you consider it too pushy if I asked if there was someone . . . a man in your life?"

"You mean Dakota's father?"

An expression of sympathy passed over his handsome features. "Hannah told me that your husband had . . . that you're widowed. I'm sorry for that, but is there someone else? You're not seeing someone or . . ."

"No." Grace shook her head. "No one,

but . . ." She hesitated. John Hartman was a terrific guy: thoughtful, funny, responsible, just the kind of person she'd want in her life . . . in her son's life. "I can't date you, if that's what you mean," she said. Why was this so hard? Why didn't he wear a wide-brimmed black hat and Amish suspenders? He would be perfect, if only . . .

"Because you're going to work for me? I can understand —" he began.

"No, it's not that," she said in a rush. "You're not Amish. I want to be Amish," she said. "So you can see, it's impossible . . . because you're not. But if you were . . ." Her cheeks grew warm and her vision blurred. "If you were, you'd be the first man I'd set my *Kapp* for."

CHAPTER EIGHT

Grace paused on the back step with a pitcher of cider in her hands and surveyed the side yard. A long table, heaped with food, stretched from the cedar tree to the rose arbor. Seated on wooden benches at either side of the table were all the men: the church elders, visitors from other Amish churches and adults from Seven Poplars. Hannah had explained to her that this was the first seating, always all-male. Younger men and teenage boys would eat at the second seating, and women and children last.

When Grace had questioned the custom, Hannah had gone on to explain that baptized men and women were considered equal in the faith, but each had their own duties and responsibilities. Seating the sexes separately at community affairs was simply the way it had always been done and maintaining tradition was a vital tenet among the

Old Order Amish.

She looked for Dakota among the pre-schoolers, didn't see him and had a moment of anxiety. But then, before she could panic, she heard her son's squeal of laughter and saw him chasing Jonah around the corner of the hen house. Dakota was running full-tilt, full of energy, as if the earlier bump to his head had never happened.

"Not to worry," Anna called, carrying a basket of bread to the table. "I told Susanna to keep the little ones away from the swing. And Lydia's big girls are watching them, too." She smiled. "Enjoy yourself. This is a day of visiting."

Grace gave a sigh of relief and smiled back. This was the way things were supposed to be, she told herself: children playing, grandmothers sharing recipes, women singing hymns as they dished up macaroni and potato salads and sprinkled cinnamon on huge bowls of applesauce. It looked like a picture from a calendar that had hung over her foster mother's desk, like a scene out of the past. An entire community had come together for a day of work and fun. This was exactly the life that she and Dakota had come so far to find.

"Grace! Men are thirsty!" Johanna's urging pulled her from her reverie.

"Coming!" Taking care not to spill the fresh cider, Grace moved toward the head of the table. Rebecca placed a bowl of chowchow on the spotless white tablecloth, glanced up and nodded her approval.

As Grace began to fill the oversize drink glasses, her thoughts were still racing. She couldn't help studying the bearded faces, trying to guess which of the men — if any — were possibilities. None of them wore wedding bands. She'd heard that there were several widowers in search of new wives, but she could hardly question her sisters or Hannah as to who they were. Her new family might think her overeager to find a man; she shouldn't, couldn't be so brazen.

There was so much she didn't know about Amish customs. It wasn't that she expected to find a husband today or even in the next few weeks. What she wanted to do, for now, was to find out what her options were. It was part of plan B. Now that she knew she wanted to become Amish, picking a new father for Dakota and a husband for herself would be the next big decision she'd have to make.

She'd hoped that cider-making day would be a perfect opportunity to survey the field, but it was going to be harder than she'd thought. Here at the first meal sitting, all the men had beards. She knew unmarried men didn't have beards. What she didn't know was whether a widower shaved his off. She hoped that they wouldn't be too old. She wasn't exactly over the hill — not yet twenty-eight — but she certainly didn't want to marry a boy barely out of his teens.

This time she was going to choose a husband logically, not because of infatuation, and she knew she was looking for a man she could respect. Friendship would be a good beginning. But when Amish men and women always separated at affairs like this, how did a single girl get to know an eligible prospect?

She smiled at a chubby brown-haired man with a neatly trimmed beard as she filled his glass with newly made cider. Instead of returning her smile, he looked embarrassed. He said something in Dutch that she couldn't understand, crammed a biscuit in his mouth and tried to wash it down with half a glass of cider. Before Grace could get away, she heard him choking.

She wanted to hide under the table. She hadn't been flirting, just being friendly. Had she broken some rule?

She backed away, and some of the cider sloshed onto her apron. Maybe he was married and he was afraid of offending her. Or maybe he was shy or . . . Grace's throat clenched. Maybe he didn't find her attractive.

Had she lost the knack of interacting with men? She'd worked as a waitress in more places than she could count, and she'd always gotten good tips, so she couldn't be awful at serving. Since Joe's death, she hadn't dated, but before they met, she'd gone out with lots of guys. She'd never had anyone so turned off that they'd almost choked to death when she'd smiled at them.

The next man was about her age, but he had a coarse black beard, bushy eyebrows, pale gray eyes and thin lips. He appeared dour, and she couldn't imagine making breakfast for him every morning for the rest of her life. When she offered him cider, he didn't speak; he just held out his glass. Grace's heart sunk as she gazed at the other men. Everyone seemed to be avoiding eye contact with her. What was she doing wrong? Why were the men so unfriendly to her? She wanted to turn and run, but she was no coward. Sucking in a deep breath, she plunged on, pouring cider for one man after the next, and having her hesitant smile met with shuttered looks or blank stares.

On the other side of the table, a tall girl with a broken front tooth laughed at something one of the men said. Rebecca had pointed her out earlier as their cousin Dorcas. Rebecca had said Dorcas was single, so that couldn't be her husband.

Grace began to wish she'd stayed in the kitchen and washed dishes. There must have been thirty men at the table, and for all she knew, they were all married except John Hartman at the far end. He sat between an older man in a denim work shirt and ball cap who didn't appear Amish and a pleasant-looking man in his early thirties with a close-cropped beard. John hadn't seemed to notice her, which was fine with her. He was the one unmarried man she had no interest in.

She nibbled on her lower lip. But maybe . . . maybe John would give her a few hints as to who was who.

Although she barely knew him, the two hours they'd spent together at the hospital this morning had increased her respect and admiration for him. He'd been good with Dakota, easing his fears, and making him laugh. And he'd done pretty much the same for her. Best of all, when the physician on call had backed up John's opinion that Dakota didn't need stitches, John didn't say, *I told you so.* Leaving the hospital, she realized that she could count John as her first friend in Seven Poplars.

She finished pouring the cider, and when her pitcher was empty, she returned to the kitchen to refill it. She checked to see that Dakota was happily playing under Susanna's watchful eye, and then returned to the yard. This time, she approached the table from the far end, offering cider first to the older man in the ball cap, then to John and then to the Amish man sitting beside him who'd caught her eye earlier. He shook his head. No.

John introduced her to his uncle Albert in the ball cap who was also a veterinarian at the clinic, and to the Amish man, Roland Byler, on his right.

Roland glanced up into her face, and his eyes widened in a look of surprise. "Welcome," he stammered. "You . . . you have the look of your sisters." He flushed, averted his eyes and reached for a piece of fried chicken.

If this one chokes, I'm out of here, Grace thought, but he didn't. She let out the breath she hadn't realized she was holding. "Pleased to meet you, Roland," she said. He was fair-haired and looked her age.

"Ya." He nodded and fixed his eyes on his plate. "And you, Grace. Good to have you here today. For the cider making."

Roland wasn't quite as handsome as John, but he had nice eyes, and an appealing laugh. Again the thought that it was just her luck that John wasn't Amish rose in her mind and she forcefully pushed it away. She'd married Joe for love, and look where that had gotten her. This time, maybe for the first time in her life, she'd have to use reason alone.

"Are you sure you wouldn't like more cider?" she asked Roland. "It's nice and cold."

"Ne." He shook his head. "Enough already. But it's *gut.* Good," he corrected. "Charley said you look like Miriam, but I think maybe like some of the others more."

Grace smiled at him encouragingly. *He was positively chatty.* She wondered if she could ask which of the women was his wife, which would tell her if he was married or if he was the good-looking bachelor some of the teenage girls had been whispering about — the bachelor with a nice farm. She tried to inspect him without being obvious. *Yes, Roland Byler definitely had possibilities.*

"Atch, sorry," Rebecca said as she rushed up and stepped on Grace's foot. Grace looked up in astonishment, and her sister shook her head. *Not him,* she mouthed silently behind Roland's back.

Grace was confused. She started to move out of the way, but Rebecca caught the corner of Grace's apron and gave a sharp tug. Grace glanced back at Roland. Thankfully, he hadn't noticed. He was busy consuming a drumstick of chicken, but John was watching her and grinning. *What have I done now?* Grace wondered.

"Mam needs you," Rebecca said loudly. "In the house." She gestured with her hand and hurried away toward the back door. Grace took the hint and followed her. Once they rounded the corner of the house, Rebecca reached for the pitcher. "I'll finish with this," she offered.

"Wait," Grace said. "I don't understand. Did I do something wrong? Is Roland Byler married?"

"Ne." Rebecca shook her head. "Not him. He was, but his wife died. A good woman, so young. The sugar."

"Sugar?" And then it dawned on her. "You mean diabetes?"

"Ya, she had the sugar. And them with a young boy."

"You mean Roland has a son?" *Like me,* she thought. *Both of us. Could that be a sign?*

"Jared. A sweet little boy." She pointed out a chubby yellow-haired child riding a stick horse on the lawn.

"I don't understand," Grace said. "Does he have a . . ." *She was going to say girlfriend, but did the Amish even have girlfriends? What was the word she'd heard used? Is he betrothed?*

"He's not walking out with anybody," Rebecca answered. "But he's not for you."

"Who's not for her?" Miriam came around the corner with a tureen of corn pudding.

"Roland Byler." Rebecca's eyes twinkled mischievously.

"Ne." Miriam looked like the cat who'd swallowed the canary. "Best you stay clear of him," she advised. And then she glanced at Rebecca and they both giggled.

"Wait," Grace protested. "Roland's single, doesn't have a girlfriend and seems pleasant. What's wrong with him?"

Rebecca stifled another chuckle. "Nothing. Roland is a nice man, everyone likes him."

"He's my husband Charley's brother," Miriam explained. "Ruth takes care of little Jared two days a week."

"Then why —" Grace began. But before she could finish, both sisters strode away toward the table, leaving her completely bewildered.

Roland leaned close to John. "Like Johanna,

she looks. Maybe not so tall, but so much. And her voice, too, like Johanna's."

John grinned. "I thought so."

Norman Beachy raised his voice from the far side of the table. "John, wonder if you'd mind stopping by my place later. I've got a sow that cut her snout on the fence. It might need stitches."

"I'd be glad to," John said. "One of your Polands?"

Norman began a long story about the pig, and John nodded, all the while considering what he'd just witnessed. Grace was checking out the men at this table, and she'd shown a real interest in Roland. John liked him. He was a good guy, an honest man, and he showed common sense and affection in dealing with his animals. Roland had even brought his son's cat in to be neutered, which endeared him to John. If country people could be persuaded to spay and neuter their pets, there'd be a lot fewer ending up dropped at the shelter. If Grace were to choose an Amish husband, she couldn't pick a better man than Roland Byler.

"Now that pig can dig under just about any fence a man can build," Norman continued. "I thought if I put down a row of cement blocks . . ."

John nodded and helped himself to another biscuit. These had to be Anna's. Her biscuits were so light they practically floated off the plate. He appreciated a good meal, and these Amish shared dinners were enough to bring tears to a bachelor's eyes. He'd spent too long suffering under Uncle Albert's attempts at imitating the chefs on television, and he himself was usually too busy to do more than throw together a grilled cheese sandwich and tomato soup.

He glanced over at Roland, wondering what Grace saw in the young farmer that she couldn't see in him. Roland was as much of a stranger to her as he was.

Women were a mystery to John. He liked to look at them, any man did, but he'd never gone out with a lot of girls. In high school, he'd been busy with sports, his part-time jobs and keeping his grades high enough to get into a good college. At university, the competition was even harder.

He'd known he wanted to be a veterinarian since he was ten years old, and his grandfather had warned him that being smart wasn't enough. He had to work hard and never lose sight of his goal. He'd met Alyssa when he was in vet school, and he'd been certain she was the one. But after she broke his heart, he hadn't been serious over any woman until Miriam.

Sometimes he wondered what was wrong with him — if he was too picky. He wanted a wife, kids, someone to share his dream home with, but after Miriam had chosen Charley, he'd let the half-finished log house he was building on the millpond stand locked and empty. He told himself that he was too busy with his practice to deal with contractors, but the truth was, without someone to share his life with, he didn't think he had the heart to complete the project. Because he didn't have the heart to think again about settling down with a woman.

Until Grace Yoder had appeared. Now, suddenly, everything was different, richer . . . brighter. The smell of the crushed apples today, the green of Grace's dress and the husky-sweet sound of her voice. He told himself that it was his imagination. She couldn't be as attractive as he imagined her, but the time they'd spent together at the hospital had made him all the more eager to see her smile at him. She might not have much formal education, but she was smart and funny and intriguing. By offering her a job at the practice, he was breaking all his own rules, but he didn't care. He wanted to spend as much time with her as he could. And if she was the woman he believed her to be, it might be that he'd want a lot more.

What was it Uncle Albert had said when he was seeing Miriam? A thunderbolt. "You've been hit by a thunderbolt, boy. It comes out of nowhere and knocks you flat. Only one woman ever made me feel like that, and she turned me down. That's why I never married."

Thunderbolt. Being with Miriam had seemed right at the time, but it hadn't been a thunderbolt, and he certainly hadn't felt like this. From the moment he'd laid eyes on Grace, he'd felt disoriented and uncertain around her . . . and himself. Maybe this was what Uncle Albert had been talking about. Whatever it was, he had no intentions of standing back and watching any Amish man, let alone Roland Byler, walk away with Grace without doing everything in his power to prevent it.

Two hours later, after the second and third sitting, John noticed Grace and her little boy come out of the house, cross the yard and enter the barn. He didn't hesitate to follow her.

Hoping that no one else was in the barn and that he'd have a few moments alone with her, John opened the door and stepped into the shadowy interior. "Grace," he called. "It's John Hartman."

"Oh, John."

His eyes adjusted to the semidarkness and he saw two figures standing by the cider-making equipment. He approached and stopped far enough away that she wouldn't get the wrong idea.

"Dakota loved the apple cider," Grace said. "He wanted to see how they make it, but . . ." She shrugged. "I suppose we should have come out earlier."

John crouched down to put himself at the boy's eye level. "How's the head, buddy?" he asked. "Does it hurt?"

Dakota shook his head. "No," he said.

"Good." John smiled at him. "You were brave, even braver than Mom."

The child offered a shy smile in return.

"So you want to know how this works?" John rose to his feet. Again, Dakota nodded. John reached under the conveyer belt and picked up a stray apple, then proceeded to explain how the apples rode up the belt, were crushed and then pressed to make the cider. "Next year, I'll make certain someone brings you out to watch," he promised.

A horse whinnied from a box stall in another section of the barn, and Dakota whipped his head around. "Can I?" he asked his mother in a small voice. "Can I see the horse?"

"Be careful," she warned. "It might bite."

"Not Molly," John answered, rubbing an apple on his pant leg. "She's a sweet old girl. And she loves apples." He took a penknife from his pocket, unfolded it and cut the apple into four pieces. He offered one to Grace.

She chuckled, accepted it and bit into it. "Delicious," she pronounced.

"Granny Smith. You can't go wrong with Granny Smith. Good for pies, applesauce, eating out of hand."

Grace walked across the straw-strewn floor to the box stall where the dapple-gray mare stood watching Dakota with large, intelligent eyes and cocked ears. Grace slid her hand into her son's small one. "Isn't she beautiful?" She glanced back at John who'd followed three steps behind. "I've always loved horses. I always dreamed of having one of my own when I was a kid."

"Do you ride?" he asked her.

"No, never learned how. Joe . . . my husband . . . He always promised to teach me, but the right day never came."

"I'm sorry. About his passing. Hannah said —"

"Joe loved the rodeo. It was his whole life. At least he died doing something he loved."

"Was the accident . . ." John trailed off. He should have had more sense than to ask for details with the boy present. Grace didn't owe him any explanations, but the way she said it . . . John looked into her eyes. She seemed sad but not grieving. He wondered how that could be possible. "How long ago?" he asked.

"It will be two years in May." She shrugged. "Dakota doesn't remember him, and sometimes . . ." She sighed. "Sometimes I can't remember his face. I try, but it keeps slipping away."

"The boy takes after him?"

She nodded. "Joe was full-blooded Native American." A muscle at the corner of her mouth tightened. "I've always been honest with Dakota. I want him to be proud of his heritage, of his father. He had his faults, but Joe was a great bronc rider. If he'd lived, he might have been a top-money winner, but our relationship wasn't always . . ." She squeezed Dakota's hand. "Like I said, rodeo meant everything to Joe."

More than his beautiful wife and son? John wondered.

"Some men aren't really meant to be tied down with a family," she added, answering his unasked question. "But if he'd lived, I know Dakota would have learned to ride.

His father would have made sure of it."

John knelt down and offered Dakota a section of apple. "You like horses, after . . ."

Grace grimaced. "Joe's accident wasn't with a horse," she said. "He was thrown from a Brahma bull. It kicked him."

John clenched his teeth. "Were you there? Did you see —"

She shook her head. "No. It was two days before one of his friends remembered where we lived. I thought he had won money and was celebrating. It wasn't unlike Joe to stay away for a week or two after a rodeo. He was in intensive care for four days before . . ."

"Look!" Dakota pointed at the mare. She was stretching her neck over the railing in an attempt to reach his piece of apple. "She wants some."

John glanced at Grace for permission and then lifted the boy and settled him on his hip. He gave him another piece of apple and showed him how to hold his hand flat. "Keep your fingers out of the way," he said. "She'll take it from you."

The mare wrinkled her nose and sniffed the apple. Then she lowered her head and gently took the treat between her teeth and munched it until the last morsel was gone. She tossed her head and blew air through her nose with a snort of sheer pleasure. Dakota giggled. "More!" he begged.

John gave him the last section, and the child held it out to the horse. Molly quickly gobbled it. "All gone," John said. "We don't want to give her a bellyache, do we? Hannah wouldn't like that."

"Ne," Dakota answered in a perfect imitation of his older cousin Jonah.

John and Grace laughed. "He's turning into a little Amish man," John said.

"Ya," Grace teased. "He is."

John hesitated, afraid to say anything that would spoil the moment. "I could teach you both," he offered.

"What?" Grace's eyes widened in curiosity. "Teach us what?"

"To ride. I have a horse, Bagherra. He's a Percheron. A really great horse."

"You have a horse?"

John chuckled. "I don't ride him often enough. I keep him at Meg Johnson's stable. She gives riding lessons, and Bagherra earns his keep by being a school horse."

"A Percheron? They're huge, aren't they?"

"Bigger than Molly, but very gentle. He'd be a perfect horse for Dakota to learn on. And I'd be glad to take you both to see him."

"We'd like that," Grace said. "So long as

Hannah thinks it's fitting."

John nodded. "We'll do it soon. Just say the day." *And I don't make promises I don't keep,* he thought.

"Can we feed your horse an apple?" Dakota asked eagerly.

"Absolutely," John said. "Two shiny red ones. He's big enough that we'll need to give him at least two."

CHAPTER NINE

Three weeks later, on a Wednesday afternoon, John and Grace left the side entrance to the veterinary clinic and walked across the parking lot to where John's truck was parked. He opened the pickup's passenger door and helped Grace climb in. "It's good of you to drive me home again," she said. "I appreciate it, but I can't keep taking advantage of you."

"You're not," he answered. He closed the door, went around to the driver's side and got behind the wheel. He'd been out earlier, so the wipers were able to easily sweep the new-fallen snow off the windshield. "I have a call at Martin's, about a mile from the Yoder farm. It was no problem to swing by the office on my way."

Grace wasn't sure that John was being entirely truthful with her. It was the third day in a row that he'd found a reason to *swing by* the office about the time Grace was getting off work, and then *happen* to be heading in the direction of the Yoder farm. She didn't want to give anyone the wrong impression by continuing to allow him to drive her home. Still, she loved every minute of her job and she didn't want to take the chance of losing it due to transportation problems. And she *did* enjoy John's company.

The plan had been for her to ride to work with Melody, one of the vet techs, in the morning and be picked up by a regular driver for the Amish in the afternoon. But the van came past the veterinary clinic around 1:00. If Grace missed that van, she couldn't catch a ride again until 5:30. And because of today's snow, traffic would be slowed and that would make her arrival at the farm even later. She had to work, but she hated being away from Dakota any longer than she had to be.

Grace settled back, fastened her seat belt and stared back at the clinic entrance. Snow had been falling since late morning, early in the year for Delaware, according to her fellow employees. The air was crisp and cold, and the parking lot, remaining cars and yard were draped in a shimmering blanket of white. Like a child, she'd always loved snow. It made everything so clean and fresh.

"Tired?" John asked. "Uncle Albert said the office was crazy today."

Grace had learned that after John's grandfather's retirement the previous year, John had continued to be on-call to care for their large-animal practice, while his uncle had started caring for cats and dogs. They had expanded their office and hired the young female veterinarian and were already thinking of hiring another. Grace got the impression that none of the men in the Hartman family had expected their small-animal practice to take off the way it had.

"I'm a little tired." She rubbed the back of her neck. She'd been up since five-thirty this morning, and they'd been so busy today that she'd barely had time to snatch a sandwich mid-afternoon. Usually, she started work at 8:00 a.m. sharp and finished by 1:00 p.m., but today everyone's schedules were off at the office.

One of the front desk clerks had called in sick, and the office had been mobbed. There had been three scheduled surgeries, a full appointment schedule, two emergencies and a sweet Rottweiler that had lost an encounter with a skunk.

Besides her usual job of cleaning cages, sweeping the kennel, feeding the animals and walking dogs, Grace had taken a turn at the desk. There, she'd answered the telephone, registered incoming patients, made and canceled appointments and collected payment for services.

"Uncle Albert said you were a huge help," John said. "He said he didn't know what they would have done without you today."

A warm wave of pleasure enveloped Grace. "It's what I'm there for, isn't it? To do whatever I can?"

"Yes, as a kennel tech, but that rarely includes the receptionist's job or dealing with skunk-sprayed animals." He grinned. "Poor Mr. O'Brien. I heard he stunk worse than his Rotti."

Grace chuckled. It was a wonder she didn't smell of skunk. Luckily, Melody had insisted she change into a jumpsuit and gloves before taking charge of poor Zeus. It wasn't one of the regular groomer's days, so bathing the animal had fallen to Grace, as well. She really hadn't minded. She loved dogs, and Zeus, despite his size, was as gentle as a lamb.

"Seriously, you're a terrific addition to the staff. Everyone agrees."

Grace smiled but kept gazing out the window. It was difficult for her to remember the plan when John was sitting so close to her. She knew that he liked her, and it would have been easy to like him, and not just as a friend. But that wasn't part of the plan. She had to keep reminding herself of that. He wasn't Amish, so all he could be to her, other than her employer, was trouble.

They were both quiet for a moment. The only sound in the cab was the swish of the windshield wipers and the crunch of the tires on the snowy road.

"You okay?" John asked, glancing her direction.

She nodded. "Fine."

He started to speak, stopped, then went on. "I . . . I don't want to make you uncomfortable, Grace. If you feel riding home with me . . ." He cleared his throat and began again. "What I'm trying to say is that you don't have to humor me to keep your job. It just seems silly for you to wait an hour and pay the driver when I can have you at Hannah's back porch in ten minutes."

Grace knew that what he was saying made sense. The van cost eight dollars a trip, and she had to watch her pennies if she didn't want to be a burden on Hannah. It wasn't that she didn't like riding with John. The truth was, she thoroughly enjoyed his company. He was fun and upbeat, and they always found interesting things to talk about. Plus, he usually had the truck radio tuned to the local country music station.

She loved country music. Music was one thing she'd really miss when she became Amish; the Amish, she'd learned, didn't permit using or listening to musical instruments. She'd have to give up her guitar, and she'd played since she was thirteen. She'd never had formal lessons, but she thought she had a real knack for it, and playing had always made her happy.

"You know I'd never do anything on purpose to make you uncomfortable."

"Of course." She turned toward him and placed a hand on his arm. "You've always been a real gentleman . . . kind to me and Dakota. I won't forget you spending half your day taking us to the hospital."

"It was the least I could do."

"No." She shook her head. "You did more than most people would. You were great. You were patient with Dakota *and* me. You told me it was just a bump, but I was being an overprotective mom. I realized that later." She shrugged. "It's just that he's all I have. I love him so much, and I can't imagine what I'd do if anything happened to him."

"He's a special little guy." He pointed with a gloved finger. "Don't forget, I did promise to give him a riding lesson. Provided it's okay with you."

Grace folded her arms, tucking her hands inside her coat sleeves. The heater was running, but she didn't have gloves, and the cab was still chilly.

She tried to think of a way to keep from hurting John's feelings. Dakota had been begging her to go and see the big horse, and she knew she would enjoy it, as well. But she was afraid that going with John would take her away from the Yoder farm, away from Hannah, her sisters and the Amish community. Not away physically — the place where John stabled the Percheron wasn't that far — but spiritually. It wasn't something an Amish woman would do. Rebecca wouldn't consider going with an *Englishman* for the afternoon. Even with Dakota along as chaperone, it might look like a date. She was still learning the ropes here, but it hadn't taken her long to figure out that the Amish cared very much how things *appeared* to their fellow church members.

Besides, seeing John, one of her bosses, after work hours might cause gossip at the clinic. And with good reason. She'd always made it a rule not to date people she worked with or for. That was a lesson she'd learned the hard way when she was eighteen and working at an ice-cream shop. She'd taken the manager, Eddy Polchak, up on an invitation for pizza and a movie and later discovered that he expected more than a thank-you for the evening. That had cost her her job, because no way was she going to compromise her sense of right and wrong, no matter how badly she needed money. She might have grown up rough, but she had standards.

Not that John would be like that. She could tell that he wasn't that kind of man.

The sad thing was, John was exactly what she was looking for, or he would have been, if he were Amish. She had a hunch that John would be an easy man to fall in love with if she was looking for love. Which she was. Just not romantic love.

For her, God's forgiveness, faith and the love of family and community had to come first. Becoming Amish was the only way she could see to make up for her past. She had to choose between a life of service and worship over a life of self. She had to choose God over the world; she believed there was mercy and peace waiting if she could step away from temptation.

Finding a solid Amish husband was part of the package, a man who lived simply and put God first in his life, a man who could guide her in the same path. Women married for lots of reasons. Some chose men who could provide them with diamond rings, big houses and fancy cars. Others picked guys for their hot looks and muscles. Grace hoped that she would be wiser. This time, she meant to find a husband best suited to fit into what she believed was God's plan for her, a man who would be a good father to her child, and one she could respect. She knew what she was looking for . . . a Plain man like . . . like Roland Byler.

The problem was, none of the Amish men seemed to notice she was alive, especially not Roland Byler. She'd seen him three times since she'd met him at the cider pressing weeks ago, but the most conversation she'd gotten out of him was a brief comment about the weather.

"Did I say something to offend you?" John asked.

"What?" Grace blinked. "I'm sorry. I was thinking about . . ." She offered him an apologetic smile. "It's not you. Really. I guess I'm under a lot of stress. Not the job," she hurried to say. "Everybody at the office has been great. It's the nicest place I've ever worked. You have a great kennel area. I love the setup and the fenced-in play area for the dogs. I just . . ."

He turned the truck off the blacktop into a farm lane and brought the vehicle to a stop. "But?" he asked.

Grace supposed she should have been alarmed, his pulling over like this, but it was John, and she wasn't afraid of him. Besides, she had to share her concerns with someone or burst.

"It's not as easy fitting into Hannah's family as I thought it would be," she blurted.

A smile played on his lips. "Or among the Amish in general?"

She nodded, slipping her hands out of her sleeves to rest them on the seat. "True."

"It's tough. I've been working in the community for almost five years and I've made a lot of friends among them. We have a lot in common. I belong to the Mennonite Church, the Amish and Mennonites spring from the same beginnings. We share a lot of the same beliefs."

She waited, sensing a *but* coming. John didn't disappoint her.

"But they *are* apart from the world. It's a tight community. Sometimes I feel welcome, sometimes I don't." He hesitated. "The fact is, Grace, they may never let you in. Not completely."

She curled her legs under her and scooted

up on the wide seat. "I know that. But it will be different for Dakota." She couldn't help smiling as she remembered how cute he looked in his little straw hat and high-top boots. "It's already different for him. You should hear him speaking Pennsylvania Dutch. And he knows the rules better than I do. We've been here only five weeks, and he's taken Hannah, Susanna, my sisters, his cousins — even *Grossmama* and Aunt Jezzy — to heart. He and Jonah are inseparable, and Dakota adores Susanna."

"What do you think of the worship services?"

Grace took a deep breath and exhaled softly. "They're long."

He grinned.

"I love the singing — it's almost like chanting. I can't understand the words, but the hymns give me goose bumps. Good ones." She closed her eyes. "You can just feel the joy in those hymns."

He let her go on.

"I understand a little Pennsylvania Dutch, and I'm picking up more every day. But the ministers read from the Bible and quote from it in High German. I'm sure I'll get more from it when my German improves."

He rubbed his gloved hand over the top of the steering wheel. "You're a brave woman, Grace. Not easily discouraged by what some would think an impossible task. Uncle Albert said he'd never heard of an Englisher successfully converting to the Old Order Amish." He shrugged. "But it could be different for you, with Hannah's help, and your sisters. I never knew your father that well, but people speak well of him. You've got that on your side, too."

"I don't know if I'll ever be able to forgive my mother for keeping me from him," she admitted. "I know that we can't expect the Lord to forgive us if we can't find forgiveness in our hearts for others. But all those years that I spent in foster care could have been so different if I'd been able to come here. Of course Jonas might not have wanted me, might have turned me away. . . ."

John reached out and brushed her hand with his gloved one. "He would have wanted you, Grace. Hannah would have wanted you. You're right. It was wrong of your mother to keep you from knowing your father and your family. She robbed you of your childhood, but she must have had her reasons."

"Not good ones. Not from where I sit. I loved her — don't get me wrong. She did the best she could, or at least she did what she thought was best for me. But it hurts so much that I never got to meet my father." She looked through the windshield at the swirling snow. "Not once."

His fingers tightened around hers. "But you have to try to forgive her. Like you said, you have to let it go. Otherwise, bitterness will poison you."

She sighed and looked back at him, pulling her hand from his. It just felt too good there. "I know, but it isn't easy." *And not just Trudie,* she thought. *I have to forgive Joe or I'll never be able to move on.*

She sat up straight and rubbed her hands briskly together. Any more of this, and she'd be blubbering like a baby. "What are you doing tomorrow for Thanksgiving?" she asked, anxious to change the subject to something less emotional. "Are you going to your mother's or spending it at home?"

"Neither. Gramps was invited to a friend's house for the day, and Uncle Albert and I will be helping members of our church serve dinner at a senior center. It's open to the entire community, but we've made a special outreach to those who might be alone or families struggling in this economy."

"That's nice. I helped at a homeless shelter once on Christmas Day. In Reno. Some of the people who came to eat were a little scary, but most were just down on their luck."

"I suppose Hannah's having a big Thanksgiving dinner with her family."

"No." Grace shook her head and sighed. "I thought so, too. The community has chosen a day of prayer and fasting this year instead of the traditional feast. Not for the children, of course. And Hannah said I could fast or not as I wanted. It's fine." She forced a chuckle. "Every day is like Thanksgiving at the Yoder table."

But it wasn't fine . . . not really. In her heart of hearts, she was disappointed. She expected this Thanksgiving to be like the ones she saw in magazines or on television. Amish-style, of course. Her throat tightened as she remembered the last Thanksgiving she and her mother had shared. There'd been takeout Chinese food in cardboard cartons, a guy named Vick who Trudie had met at a truck stop, a buddy of Vick's and thay guy's girlfriend. The adults had gotten into an argument, then a fistfight, and Grace had ended up hiding in a closet. What had hurt most was that her mother hadn't even missed her, and when Grace finally crawled out of the dark, everyone, including Trudie, had left.

"I'm going to fast with them," she said

determinedly. "It's just from after supper tonight until tomorrow night. Then we'll have bread and broth. I'm sure it will be a good experience."

"It is. It's not something my church does often, but I've taken part in fasting before." His gaze met hers. "Did you belong to a church? Before you came here, I mean? I hope you don't mind my asking," he added quickly.

"Not a problem." She gave a wave. "Trudie was never one for churchgoing. But my foster mother, the one with the dogs, never let us miss a Sunday. I got in the habit. I moved around a lot, but I liked to attend church whenever I could. I went to lots of different denominations, but I can't say that I really belonged anywhere."

He hesitated and then backed the truck out of the lane onto the road. "I'd better get you home. They'll be wondering where I am. My appointment, I mean."

"Yes," she agreed.

They rode the rest of the way to the Yoder drive in companionable quiet. As he turned into the dirt lane, John said, "Our church has an open invitation to visitors. We could use help serving tomorrow for Thanksgiving, and naturally, you'd be welcome at any worship service . . . if the Amish . . ."

"Thank you," she said, putting her hand on the door handle. She opened the door as the truck came to a stop, just yards from Hannah's back gate. "I would love to help with the dinner, but I couldn't leave Dakota on Thanksgiving Day."

"You could bring him," John suggested, sounding disappointed. "The volunteers from our church always include their kids in our activities."

"I don't think so, but thanks for offering." She climbed out. "Thanks again for the ride home." She didn't look back until she got to the porch. He waved, and she waved back, then stamped her feet to get the snow off before she went into the house.

"I'm home," she called as she stepped into the warm kitchen. She didn't see Dakota or any of the children, but Hannah, Aunt Jezzy, Johanna, Rebecca and Susanna were all there, gathered around the table. Hannah had been speaking, but she bit off her words in mid-sentence.

Everyone looked at Grace.

The nape of Grace's neck prickled as thoughts of John flew out of her head. Hannah's features strained with obvious distress. Not once — not even on the evening she and Dakota had arrived — had she felt so much discord in this room. "What is it?"

Grace asked. "Are the children all right? Dakota —"

"Fine." Hannah's voice was uncharacteristically tight. "Playing in the front parlor. Irwin is watching them."

Irwin? What had happened that none of them wanted the children to hear what they were discussing? And what was so important that Irwin would be pressed into babysitting while Grace's sisters, including Susanna, were here? Grace studied the faces she'd come to know so well. Even Aunt Jezzy had traded her sweet smile for pursed lips and a troubled expression. "Have I done something?" Grace asked, afraid they had been waiting for her. Lying in wait even.

"Ne." Hannah shook her head. "Not at all."

"It's private," Johanna said. "Just family."

Grace shrugged off her coat and hung it on a hook. "I am family," she said. Her knees felt weak, but she wouldn't be dismissed so easily. "Whether you like it or not, little sister. I'm here and I care about you all. Anything that worries all of you concerns me."

"Ya," Aunt Jezzy agreed. She motioned to the empty place beside her. "You see that look in her eyes, Hannah, my brother's look." She glanced at Johanna, speaking in English. "Shame on you. Now, more than

ever, we must draw close together. And you cannot deny that she is your father's child and your elder."

Johanna's face flushed but she nodded. "I'm sorry, Grace," she murmured. "I'm just upset." She nodded toward their youngest sister. "It's our Susanna. And David King."

Susanna? What could Susanna have done wrong? Grace wondered as she looked across the table at her youngest sister. Susanna's cheeks were redder than Johanna's, and her bottom lip protruded in a stubborn pout.

"Aunt Jezzy found Susanna and David on the stairs," Hannah explained. "Behaving in an inappropriate way."

Grace knew her eyes must have widened in surprise. *Susanna and David King? What had they been doing that upset everyone? Susanna was Susanna, and David, although he was older, seemed even more of a child.*

"Making mischief." Aunt Jezzy lifted her graying eyebrows. "The two of them."

"King David is not bad. He's good." Susanna's eyes crinkled up. Her pout faded and her chin quivered. "I love him."

"No," Hannah said gently. "David's not bad. No one said that. Neither of you is bad."

Johanna slipped an arm around Susanna's shoulder. "He's not bad. Only unwise."

Hannah whispered to Grace behind her hand. "They were kissing."

But Susanna heard. "I did!" Susanna shouted. "I did kissed King David," she said. "I love him." She nodded vigorously. "King David and me." Her mouth spread into a wide smile. "I kissed him because we're getting married."

CHAPTER TEN

"There will be no more kissing between you and David," Hannah admonished, waggling her finger. "David is a friend, not family. We don't kiss friends or strangers who are boys. And you aren't old enough to get married."

"Am, too! Ada-Ann said so," Susanna flung back. She threw up all ten fingers. "I had my birthday. I'm nineteen. And . . . and King David is . . . is . . ." She seemed to struggle with her thoughts for a moment. "He's old!"

"He's twenty-three," Johanna mouthed to Grace.

"I know Ada-Ann is your friend," Rebecca calmly told Susanna. "But she isn't your mother. She doesn't know everything. And Mam says you're too young."

"But . . . I love King David." Susanna giggled. "He kisses good."

"You were kissing David, Susanna?" Grace asked, more to calm the situation than to clarify. "On the cheek or on the lips?"

Susanna patted her mouth with two fingers and giggled again.

"You see," Aunt Jezzy declared, throwing up her skinny arms. "She's an innocent. Susanna isn't even ashamed of it."

"She doesn't understand," Rebecca told Aunt Jezzy, "but she will if you explain it carefully." She smiled at her younger sister. "*Plain* girls only kiss boys *after* they are married, Susanna."

"Irwin kissed a girl at Spence's. Sunday." Susanna bounced in her seat. "An Englisher girl. I saw him."

Grace tried not to laugh. If *that* were true, Irwin was in trouble. But it couldn't have happened on Sunday because the auction was closed on Sundays. Susanna didn't have a strong grasp of the order of the days of the week. When she related any incident, she always said it happened on Sunday.

Hannah rolled her eyes. "If Irwin did kiss a girl, that was wrong. I'll have a talk with him, but we're not talking about Irwin right now, we're talking about you, Susanna. You are *not* allowed to kiss David anymore."

"But . . . but we're getting married," Susanna insisted. "Sunday."

"Not this Sunday," Grace soothed, rising from her chair to stroke her sister's arm.

She glanced at Hannah, who nodded approval, and then back to Susanna. "It takes a long time. First Bishop Atlee has to give his permission, then Mam and David's parents."

"And bans have to be read for weeks at worship service," Rebecca put in.

Hannah looked up at the clock and clapped her hands together. "Goodness, look at the time." She rose. "Girls, set the table. The children must be starving."

"But Mam . . ." Susanna whined. "I want —"

"You heard Grace. It takes a long time to get married. Now be a good girl and get the knives and forks." Hannah headed for the stove. "Johanna made *ob'l dunkes kucka* and that's your favorite."

"Molasses shoo-fly cake!" Susanna clapped her hands. "King David likes cake!"

The Saturday morning after Thanksgiving, Johanna and Grace sat at a table in the crowded dining area of Spence's Bazaar, a bargain-sale, auction and Amish market, and watched as Rebecca bought Jonah and Dakota ice-cream cones. Katie had remained home with Ruth and Susanna, while the two little boys enjoyed an outing with their mothers and Aunt Rebecca.

The boys loved going to Spence's, and so did Grace. Here in the food building were Amish booths with all kinds of delicious foods, from Lancaster specialty cheeses to ham, bacon, sausage and all kinds of tasty deli meats. There were candies, jams and a bakery where the children could watch Amish girls with muscular arms, red cheeks and starched *Kapps* pull trays of fragrant yeast bread and cinnamon rolls hot from the oven.

The air smelled of hamburgers, apple pie, pizza and gingerbread. Everywhere Amish and non-Amish chatted, ate and shopped, and the guttural Pennsylvania Dutch dialect was as commonly heard as English.

Now that the children were away from the lunch table, Johanna picked up an earlier conversation concerning Susanna and David's kissing incident. "Mam worries," Johanna confided. "We've never expected to have anything like this happen with her. Susanna has always been such an easy child . . . a good girl."

"And she's still a good girl," Grace defended. "But she's almost twenty. She may have a more difficult time learning than the rest of us, but in some ways, she's a normal teenager." She shrugged. "She must have the same thoughts and feelings as any young woman. Why does your mother treat her differently than she does Rebecca?"

Johanna's mouth firmed. "Because she *is* different."

"Yes, Susanna is different." Grace nodded. "For me, not because she was born with Down's, but because she was the first one to accept Dakota and me. She has such a pure heart."

"I agree with you that our little sister is one of God's special children," Johanna replied, "but realistically, Susanna has limits. One of us will always have to care for her. It's not a burden. We love Susanna, but we know what must be. And she can't go around kissing boys because she likes the way it feels."

"Of course not." Grace took Johanna's hand and squeezed it affectionately. "Rebecca wouldn't be allowed to behave like that, either, would she?"

Johanna's expression softened. "*Ne*. But Rebecca knows what is modest behavior and what isn't. And then, of course, there's an issue of safety."

Grace nodded, knowing all too well that a young woman could get herself into trouble kissing the wrong man. Hadn't she made that very same mistake with Joe?

"Susanna doesn't have the ability to make

164

those kinds of judgments," Johanna added.

"Maybe not, but maybe it's just because she's been too sheltered. When you look at her, what do you see? A little girl?" Grace leaned forward. "I don't. I see a beautiful young woman, not beautiful in the way that Rebecca and you are beautiful, but . . ." She thought back to the first time she'd laid eyes on Susanna, and how pleasantly surprised she'd been. "I don't know how to put it, but Susanna just glows. Her eyes sparkle with a special inner light."

"*Ya.*" Johanna admitted. "They do. We have all seen it."

"So why can't Susanna do the things that other girls her age do, that Rebecca does? Why can't she go to singings and young people's outings? Properly chaperoned, of course. Why can't she talk to nice Amish boys her own age and share secrets with girlfriends like every other teenager?"

Johanna's flawless brow furrowed and she absently wound a bonnet string around one finger. "Susanna does go to singings and work frolics."

"She told me that she always has to carry the pie basket, sit by the cookies and pour lemonade. Like a *grossmama.* She says that she never gets to play games like the other girls — or ride home alone with boys in their father's buggies."

"Susanna told you that? When?" Johanna seemed genuinely surprised. "When did she say such things?"

"Thanksgiving Day. We were talking when we fed the chickens and gathered the eggs. She confided in me. She said everyone thinks she's a baby and she's not."

"Atch . . ." Compassion flooded Johanna's eyes. "I never knew Susanna felt that way. She seems so happy, like a —"

"Like a child?" Grace supplied. "But she's not, is she?"

"But . . ." Johanna scrambled to respond. "She can't ever marry, have children, manage a household."

Grace shrugged. "All the more reason she should have the fun of being a teenager, don't you think?"

"I suppose . . ."

"Aunt Jezzy never married, did she?" Grace asked. "But I'm sure she had her *rumspringa* years. Probably even had a radio hidden in the hayloft to listen to Elvis."

Johanna's gaze met Grace's, and both started to giggle at the thought of sedate Aunt Jezzy rebelling against her parents' teachings.

"Mam! Mam! I got choc'late!" Dakota dodged an English woman in a blue polka-dot dress and skidded to a stop beside the table. His face was already smeared with chocolate ice cream, and he was grinning so hard that a dimple appeared on his cheek.

"I see you did," Grace answered with a smile. She glanced back at Johanna. "Just think about what is best for Susanna and talk to your mother."

"About Susanna?" Rebecca asked, joining her sisters.

Johanna nodded.

"Well, at least Susanna isn't marrying David *this* Sunday. Sadie told Mam that she and David were going to spend a few days at her daughter's house."

Johanna successfully dodged an ice-cream drip as she lifted Jonah and his strawberry cone onto her lap. "The Kings will have their new roof on their house before Christmas and they'll be moving in. I'm sure Susanna will forget all about this getting married to David. You know how she is."

"I do know how she is." Rebecca took a seat. "That's the problem. Sometimes, Susanna latches onto an idea and holds it like a squirrel to a stolen acorn."

Jonah and Dakota both laughed. "I like squirrels," Dakota said. "I want Santa to bring me a squirrel. Not a cartoon squirrel, a real one. And a train, one that blows smoke and has a whistle and —"

"What's a cartoon squirrel?" Jonah asked.

"Secret Squirrel." Dakota licked at a drip of chocolate. "On TV."

Jonah wrinkled his nose and glanced up at his mother. "Secret Squirrel?"

"He's never watched television," Johanna explained to Dakota.

"Ask Santa to bring you one," Dakota urged Jonah.

Rebecca looked uncomfortable. "There was a man dressed up like Santa Claus by the ice cream. Dakota wanted to tell him where he lived now."

"So he doesn't miss me. And forget to bring toys." He waved his cone at Jonah for emphasis. "Last year he brought a Christmas tree and a fire truck with a bell and —"

"Who is Santa Claus?" Jonah tilted his head and looked up at his mother. "Will he bring me a fire truck?"

Johanna's mouth opened and closed. Then she shook her head. "*Ne*, Jonah, Santa Claus is for Englishers. He doesn't come to Plain children, just English houses."

"But I'm English," Dakota protested. "Irwin said so. Englisher, he said."

Jonah nodded. "He did. But Irwin also said there was trolls under the chicken house. And *Grossmama* said Irwin was a *dummkopp* and trolls live far away in Belleville."

"*Dummkopp*," Dakota echoed with a giggle.

"Not a word for little boys," Johanna chided. "It was unkind to say, even about Irwin. He isn't a dunce, just *verhuddelt.* Mixed up," she translated for Grace. "No trolls here *or* in Pennsylvania."

And no Santa Claus, either, Grace thought sadly. That was a beloved tradition that she and Dakota would have to give up . . . and that might be even more painful than surrendering her guitar. *I hope I'm doing the right thing. It has to be,* she thought. *I've prayed and prayed, and I can't think of any other way to make up for what I've done.* She was just sorry that Dakota would have to pay the price, too.

Rebecca passed out ham-and-cheese sandwiches that she'd purchased. "I hope you like mustard."

"We do," Grace assured her.

Johanna had found a book of old quilt patterns in one of the thrift shops and was anxious to show it to Rebecca. As everyone ate and talked, Grace found her thoughts drifting away and reflecting on the weeks since she'd come to live at Seven Poplars.

As both Hannah and John had warned, it

was a struggle for her to fit into the Amish lifestyle. Dakota had adapted quickly, but as much as she reveled in having family and a warm and joyous home, she was still torn between this new life and her old one. She loved the quiet nights in the snug farmhouse without the blare of highway traffic or the shouts of feuding neighbors. She loved the shared dinners and the animals and the slower pace of life. But she loved her job at the veterinary clinic, as well.

She found being part of the practice exciting. She liked chatting with the drug reps, placing orders for cleaning supplies and socializing with the clients. Lunch with her fellow employees was fun, and she found herself drawn to several of the vet techs, enjoying the camaraderie and the shop talk. She liked the Christian radio station that played in the waiting room and in the kennel area. And most of all, she loved watching everyone caring for sick and injured animals, and the feeling that she was a valuable piece of the puzzle. Every day brought something new to learn, and every day . . . despite her efforts not to, she found herself watching and hoping for glimpses of John. Even though, as the large-animal vet for the practice, he was on the road much of his day, she never knew when he might stop by for supplies or just to see how everyone was getting along, as he put it.

She had to stop riding home with him. She knew it. The more time she spent alone with John, the worse it would be when she had to let him go. He wasn't part of her future, and becoming attached to him was a wrong turn on the path God had planned for her. Next time John offered, she would simply decline.

"But you can't say no. You'll have to go," Rebecca said, breaking into Grace's musing.

Grace's eyes widened and she blinked. *Had she spoken John's name aloud?* "Excuse me?"

"You'll have to go with Susanna," Johanna explained. "To the corn-husking work frolic at Lydia and Norman Beachy's house next Saturday. To be her chaperone."

"Me?" Grace asked, still trying to catch up with the conversation. "A husking frolic?"

"*Ya.*" Rebecca chuckled. "It will be fun. There will be a bonfire and games. And husking heaps of feed corn for the Beachys. They always have more work than they can manage alone."

"There will be young people," Johanna said pointedly. "A few older couples who act as chaperones, but mostly unmarried. The Amish don't allow their teens and young adults to date, so it's how they meet and decide who to court."

"But you said Susanna . . ." Grace looked from one to the other and lowered her voice when she noticed an Amish woman at another table watching them with interest. "She wouldn't be allowed . . ."

"Susanna will go for the games and the food," Johanna clarified. "But you will go to look for a husband. It's the perfect opportunity."

"A good Amish boy," Rebecca added. "You want one, don't you? This is how we choose."

"Aren't I a little old for boys?" Grace asked.

Rebecca snickered. "Men, then." She glanced at Johanna and then back to Grace. "I'm sure Roland Byler will be there, and he's nearly thirty. Maybe Johanna should go with us, too."

Johanna looked down at Jonah and stood up. "Sticky hands. We'll have to get these two boys to the washroom."

"Of course, if Susanna . . ." Grace looked from one sister to the other. Rebecca had a positively mischievous gleam in her eyes. "Will Hannah let her go?" Grace asked.

"Probably," Johanna said.

"I'm sure she will." Rebecca spread her hands, palm up and smiled. "What harm could there be with her oldest sister there to watch over her?"

A week later, Grace shared the front seat of the Yoder family buggy with Rebecca and Susanna as they rolled along the blacktop in the brisk darkness. It was a clear, crisp December night, with stars as bright as diamonds and a huge harvest moon. The three of them were well bundled up with scarves, capes and mittens. Rebecca drove the horse called Blackie.

Grace hoped that she wouldn't do or say anything that made her look foolish tonight. She had no idea what a husking frolic was or how she would tell which of the Amish men were available and which weren't. Maybe the best thing to do was to wait for them to approach her. They all certainly knew who she was.

As they approached the Beachy farm, Grace saw four other buggies ahead of them on the road. "A good lot tonight," Rebecca said, flicking the reins over Blackie's back. The horse broke into a trot, and Grace grasped the edge of the seat. "You know I was teasing Johanna the other day about

Roland Byler," Rebecca said as they entered the lane.

"Yes?" Grace urged.

"He won't really be there. Even if he was, he isn't right for you."

"You said that before. But why? He seems nice."

"Johanna and Roland used to walk out together," Rebecca explained. "Before she married Wilmer." She shrugged. "Johanna says the last thing she wants is another husband right now, but who knows?"

"Johanna likes Roland," Susanna said. "Anna said so."

Rebecca chuckled. "And *that,* Susanna banana, is a secret. Don't say it to anybody, especially not Johanna." She reined in the horse near the barn, and a tall, gangly young man came to take the horse's halter. "Vernon, this is our sister Grace," Rebecca said. "You'll have to help introduce her to the others. Grace, Vernon Beachy."

He mumbled something, but before Grace could return the greeting, another figure moved out of the shadows with a familiar rolling gait. Susanna squealed. "King David! Hi!" He laughed and waved, and Susanna scrambled down from the buggy.

"Good luck," Rebecca said with a chuckle. "It looks like you have your chaperone work cut out for you tonight."

Keeping up with Susanna and David should have been easy, and it was while they were all in the barn during the corn husking and the clapping games and singing. Susanna played and won what Grace supposed was an Amish version of musical chairs with hay bales substituted for chairs. But once the frolic moved outside to the bonfire and refreshments, it was almost impossible to not lose one blue dress and black bonnet in a crowd of black bonnets and blue dresses.

There must have been three dozen teenagers, all laughing, jostling and teasing one another amid the roasting of hot dogs and toasting of marshmallows. Susanna and David seemed to be having the time of their lives, but once either of them stepped back from the circle of firelight, they were quickly lost in the shadows and Grace found herself having to gently encourage them to join the others again.

Grace had determined in the first twenty minutes that other than good-looking Mordecai Miller and determined Barnabas Swartzentruber, who were both doing their best to charm Rebecca, there wasn't another unmarried male over the age of twenty-one. Grace's hopes of meeting someone —

anyone — had swiftly faded and been wholly replaced by a determination to not allow Susanna the opportunity for any more mischief.

The only person she'd had any exchange of conversation with all evening had been her sister Miriam who'd come with her husband, Charley, to help the host and hostess of the frolic. But there hadn't been much opportunity to talk with Miriam, either, because she had been busy passing out refreshments. Charley, in the meantime, had been busy policing the frolic. He had confiscated two radios, an iPod and a cell phone, and had sent two boys home after he'd witnessed them poking fun at David King.

"Stutzman brothers. Not from our church district," Charley said, as the guilty party drove their horse and buggy hastily down the lane. "But they should know better. Ananias Stutzman is a deacon. Wait until I tell him how his sons behaved. They'll be shoveling manure until Pentecost Monday."

Grace was easing her way into the throng of teenagers around the bonfire when she heard the rumble of wagon wheels and the clip-clop of hooves in the farmyard. She glanced over her shoulder to see a hay wagon pulled by two enormous draft horses. Driving the animals was a man in a black felt cowboy hat and a thick denim jacket. She couldn't see his face, but something looked very familiar about him, so familiar that her heart skipped a beat.

"Look who's here," Miriam said, appearing at Grace's shoulder.

Charley, approaching them, laughed. "I'm guessing that's her ride home."

"Me?" Grace asked, thoroughly confused.

"Grace Yoder!" the man in the cowboy hat shouted, much to the amusement of the teens and young adults gathered around the dying bonfire. "Would you do me the honor?" He swept off the wide-brimmed hat, and there was no longer any doubt as to his identity.

Grace couldn't help laughing. It was John Hartman.

Chapter Eleven

"Grace Yoder! Will you ride home in my courting buggy?" John shouted, to the delight of the audience who all laughed and cheered. He spread his arms wide and swept his cowboy hat dramatically into the air.

Grace wanted to crawl under the nearest bale of hay. Her cheeks burned with embarrassment. Pulse racing, she turned away, hoping to hide in the crowd, but Susanna caught her elbow.

"Look, Grace!" Susanna's round face glowed with excitement in the firelight.

Grace pulled away from her.

"It's John! With . . . with Samuel's horses! Can we come? Please? Can King David and me ride in the hay wagon?" Susanna tugged at a chubby hand, and David King appeared from the crowd, clutching an unopened two-liter bottle of soda to his chest, his prize for winning one of the clapping games. David rarely spoke, but his eager, smiling face said it all. He wanted to go as much as Susanna did.

"I'm not riding home with John," Grace protested. But, oh, how she wanted to. It was so romantic, John coming for her in Samuel's wagon. And it was fun. Innocent. Unlike much of the Englisher ways of dating. And to think, John would do it in front of the whole young community of Seven Poplars. He must really like her.

The temptation was so great that Grace could feel it urging her toward the wagon. No, that feeling of being propelled forward, she realized, that wasn't temptation. It was Rebecca and two of her girlfriends pushing her forward through the group.

"Go on," Rebecca urged.

Grace planted her feet. "I can't."

Rebecca glanced at her friends and the three giggled.

"Is this a setup?" Grace asked suspiciously. "Did you know John was going to do this?" She'd been chilly earlier, but now she felt as if she'd been standing too close to the fire.

Rebecca shook her head. "*Ne,* but if you take Susanna and David with you, it would be good." She smiled mischievously. "Then, I can ride home with . . . with someone else."

The two girls beside her, neither of whom

Grace knew, chuckled again. "Maybe Barney," the tallest girl said. Her black bonnet shadowed her face, but Grace could see a delicate dimpled chin and pretty mouth.

"Or Mordecai Miller." The other young woman, both shorter and plumper, nudged Rebecca. "They *both* asked her," she whispered.

Rebecca clapped a hand over her mouth and snickered. "Shh. You're not supposed to tell."

"Everybody knows," the tall girl said. "Mordecai told Mahlon that Barney didn't stand a chance of you riding home with him."

Rebecca threw Grace a pleading look.

"Rebecca . . . Don't do this to me," Grace begged, but it was too late. Charley and Miriam were both urging her to accept John's offer, too. And then the crowd parted, and John was standing in front of her, cowboy hat in hand, grinning sheepishly.

John leaned close to her. "You have to come, Grace," he said softly. "I'll never live it down in the community if you don't. Everyone will laugh at me forever."

"I don't *have* to do anything," she retorted. She couldn't do it. She didn't have the luxury of following her heart — not even for an evening. She had to think of Dakota and what was best for the two of them.

"We want to ride in the hay wagon," Susanna repeated. "Don't we, King David?" David nodded so vigorously that his bottle of soda slid out of his hands and would have fallen to the ground if John hadn't grabbed it in midair and returned it safely to him.

"I'll bet you've never been on a hayride," John teased Grace. "How can you refuse the opportunity?"

How could he know? Grace wondered. A long-buried memory flashed in her mind, a snapshot of her standing at the third-story bedroom window on a Saturday night and watching a hay wagon of singing teenagers roll by the driveway of her foster home.

The hayride was the highlight of football quarterback Bill McNamara's birthday party, and he'd asked her to be his date. It was the first time he'd noticed her, and she'd wanted desperately to go. But even though she begged, her foster mother had refused permission. The 9:00 p.m. lights-out rule was inflexible, and there would be church at 8:30 in the morning, with kennel and house chores and breakfast starting at 6:00 a.m. She'd cried herself to sleep that night, and on Monday, Bill and Amy Pierson were an item. No, she'd never gotten her hayride . . . and deep inside, it still hurt.

"*Ya!*" Elmer Beachy shouted. "Go with him!" A dozen other teenagers chimed in, all clapping and yelling. "Ride with him, Grace Yoder."

Would Susanna be as disappointed as she had been if she didn't get to go in the hay wagon tonight? Would Rebecca be upset with Grace if she didn't give her the opportunity to ride home alone with a boy? Was she being as inflexible as her foster mother by putting rules ahead of someone's happiness? Grace glanced at Miriam. "If I agree, I can take Susanna," she said. "But how can I take responsibility for David? His mother might not want him to go. Is he here with someone? It wouldn't be right for me to —"

"It's all right," John assured her. "I already asked his parents. The Kings are sleeping at Hannah's again tonight. Sadie and Ebben gave their permission." John flashed a triumphant grin. "And so did Hannah."

"You mean everyone knows about this ambush but me?" Grace protested. She could feel her resolve weakening. It was only a ride in a wagon with a friend. What harm could it do? She glanced again toward the restless team.

The big horses stamped their hooves, tossed their manes and blew clouds of warm breath into the cold air. What a shame it would be if John had brought them out for nothing. "All right," she agreed. "I'll ride with you *this* time." *But no more,* she vowed. *This is the last time I go anywhere with John Hartman. I'll have my hayride, but after that, I'll find a way to convince John that there's no chance for us.*

The teenagers followed them to the wagon, some clapping, others still catcalling and teasing in Pennsylvania Dutch. But it was all in good fun; nothing was mean or hurtful. Susanna and David followed close on their heels, not wanting to be left behind.

Grace supposed she should have been angry at John. This was preposterous. What was wrong with him that he couldn't take no for an answer? Why couldn't he accept the idea that she wasn't interested in going out with him? Why couldn't he understand that she only wanted him as a friend?

Because it's not true, she thought. A little catch in the back of her throat made her swallow. Coming for her with a hay wagon and a pair of magnificent Percherons was the most romantic thing any guy had ever done for her — like something out of a movie. And how did he guess that she'd always had a thing for men in cowboy hats? John didn't play fair.

"John Hartman, I'll get even with you for

this," she whispered as he caught her by the waist and swung her up into the wagon. "You'll be sorry."

"I hope not," he answered.

Young men and women crowded around the wagon. Someone boosted David King up, and then Charley and Norman Beachy helped Susanna. She tumbled into the loose straw, scrambled up, laughed and clapped her hands together.

Rebecca brought an extra blanket from the buggy and wrapped it around Susanna's shoulders. "So you won't catch a chill," she said. And then she leaned close and whispered. "And remember what Mam said. No kissing."

Susanna glanced at David, and hugged herself tightly. "No kissing," she repeated and giggled again. David, still holding his bottle of soda proudly, plunked himself on a bale of straw and grinned back at Susanna.

Grace saw Mordecai standing behind Rebecca. *I suppose it's only fair,* Grace thought. *Rebecca should be allowed to ride home with the boy of her choice. She shouldn't have to babysit me and Susanna all the time. If doing this made both Susanna and Rebecca happy, it had to be the right thing, didn't it?*

John waved Grace to a bale beside him,

tugged his hat down tightly on his head and gathered the leather lines in his hands. Charley backed the team and led the horses in a wide circle. "You and Miriam be good now," John said as he flicked the reins lightly over the Percherons' broad backs. "Remember, married or not, you two need to set a good example."

Charley laughed and called to the team, "Walk on." Susanna gave a small squeal of joy as the wagon lurched forward and rolled across the farmyard toward the lane. "No kissing! Any of you!" Charley shouted, and everyone laughed again.

"Very funny," Grace said to John under her breath. "I hope you've enjoyed your little joke."

"Not a joke," John answered good-naturedly. "How else was I supposed to get a date with you?"

"This is *not* a date," she said.

He chuckled. "You keep telling yourself that, Grace."

Balancing herself with both hands on a bale of straw, Grace turned around so that she was facing the back of the wagon and could see Susanna and David.

Susanna looked up and smiled. "It's wonderful," she proclaimed. David nodded but he didn't take his gaze off Susanna.

Noting that there was a decent distance between the two, Grace slid around and gave her attention to John. "You weren't exactly truthful with me."

"Me? How so?"

"You told me that it was a hayride," she said with a straight face. "I don't see any hay. All I see are bales of straw."

He groaned and clutched his chest. "You got me. Hayride just sounded better than straw ride. And you wouldn't want hay if you've ever sat on it."

She laughed. "I suppose I can forgive you for that, but I wanted you to know that I know the difference. I did grow up out west. Lots of hay out there."

"And straw?" he teased.

"And straw," she agreed. When they reached the end of the Beachys' drive, they turned right instead of left. "I thought you were taking us home," she said.

"I am, but it would be a shame to get these horses all hitched up and not give them proper exercise. I didn't say what route we were taking." He winked. "An old Amish trick." He guided the team a hundred feet and then crossed the road and took a dirt logging road. "Keep your eyes out for deer," he called to Susanna and David. "Samuel said there have been a lot of them

186

this winter."

"Are you a hunter?" Grace asked.

Joe had been a hunter, and she'd always hated it when he'd brought home a kill. But the game had often been the only meat she could put on the table for the family. Joe didn't work much in winter and her paychecks went for rent, gas and car insurance for both of them. Hunting had kept them from public assistance, and for that she'd been grateful. Still, she'd always felt sorry for the animals.

"I shoot a lot of wildlife," John said. "With a camera, especially birds. I fish a little, but no hunting. I enjoy watching the animals too much."

"What kind of camera do you use?" She was interested. Joe had bought her an inexpensive digital camera for Christmas one year, and she'd taken pictures of Dakota when he was a baby. The camera had gotten lost in one of their moves, and she'd never had the extra money to replace it. Now, she supposed she never would. The Amish didn't allow photographs to be taken of themselves. Hannah had explained that the Bible warned against making graven images.

John began to tell her about his camera, and her last bit of annoyance at being coerced into riding home with him fell away.

They laughed and talked, and when they finally turned into Hannah's lane, she realized that she was sorry the evening was over.

"Thanks for coming with me," John said as he brought the horses to a halt in front of the house. "It was the best first date I've ever had."

"I had fun, too," she admitted, "but it *wasn't* a date."

"Oh yes, it was." He was still teasing, but there was something else in his tone, something she didn't want to contemplate.

"No, it wasn't," she insisted, getting in the last word as she popped up off the bale of straw. But as she jumped down from the wagon without waiting for John's assistance, she suspected that he was right. That was exactly what it was — an unforgettable date that threw a giant monkey wrench into her plans for the future.

The following afternoon, a visiting Sunday, John parked his truck near the Yoders' back gate, got out and walked toward the house. The previous night's surprise hayride had gone better than he'd hoped. Once he had Grace in the wagon, she hadn't held a grudge for the underhanded way he'd landed their first date. She'd laughed and talked, and she'd drawn Susanna and David into the conversation so that they wouldn't feel left out, and, he supposed, they wouldn't do anything of which anyone's mother would disapprove.

Grace's kindness to Susanna and David and her obvious affection for her younger sister had eased the way into his next suggestion. Once a month, on Sunday afternoon, after services, volunteers from his Mennonite church took mentally and physically challenged teenagers bowling. The event ended with pizza at one of the local restaurants. He'd wanted to invite Susanna, and Hannah had seemed open to the idea, but she'd been reluctant to allow her daughter to go because there were no other Amish attending.

This time, he'd asked Grace first, and she'd agreed to speak to Hannah and David's parents. And as he'd hoped, Grace offered to come and help out, so long as she could bring her son with her. Both families had thought that it would be a wonderful opportunity for their children.

Apparently, David had left friends behind in the Kings' old community, and his parents were eager for him to be happy here in Seven Poplars. Broadening Susanna's and David's world was something that John felt good about, but spending more time with Grace was icing on his cake.

The back door to the farmhouse opened and David ambled out, one prong of his battered cardboard crown sticking out from under his straw hat. Susanna came next, with a smiling Grace bringing up the rear.

"Where's Dakota?" John asked as he assisted David into the front seat and the two young women into the one behind. "He's not coming?"

"Toad in his head," Susanna replied.

"A cold," Grace clarified. "No fever, but Dakota was sneezing, and because the temperature is hovering around freezing, I thought he would be better if he stayed home where it's warm."

"I'm glad you didn't wake up with a cold," John told Grace.

"What? And let these two go off on their own?" Grace chuckled. "Hannah made me promise to watch over them like a banty hen with two chicks."

Susanna sat tall and straight on the seat. Instead of her *Kapp,* Hannah had sent her off with a navy blue wool scarf tied over her braided and pinned-up hair. She wore a robin's egg blue dress, a black cape, black apron and black stockings. Her sturdy leather shoes were polished to a high gleam.

"And who is this?" John teased.

Susanna giggled. "You know me," she answered. "Susanna."

David nodded and grinned. "Susanna," he echoed.

John closed the doors and went around the front of the truck. He climbed in behind the wheel. "And you're David King?" he asked, pointing at David.

"King David," Susanna corrected.

John glanced in the rearview mirror at Grace. She shrugged and chuckled. "Right," John said. "King David. I forgot."

David turned on the radio and kept pushing buttons until Christian music poured from the speakers. He nodded and sighed, settling back and tapping time to the music on the door as a group poured forth a joyous song of praise.

John met Grace's gaze in the mirror again, and she nodded her approval. "Perfect," she agreed, as David began to hum along.

By the time they reached the bowling alley, others had already arrived. John introduced Grace, David and Susanna to church volunteers Caroline and Leslie Brown, who were assisting two young people to find the correct size bowling shoes. "These are Daniel's cousins," he explained. "Your sister Leah's husband."

Once introductions were made, Kyle Stoffel, the church youth leader, and his cousin Evan Cho, took charge of David and took him to check his coat and hat and find shoes. Grace offered to keep score, and the group moved to the two bumpered lanes set aside for them.

Susanna quickly made friends with Amelia and Destiny. Susanna's bowling skills were sorely lacking, but that didn't curb her enthusiasm. David, on the other hand, turned out to be the best bowler of the group, easily scoring higher than the girls or the other two boys, much to his delight. His newfound friends admired his crown, as well, and the accolades made his chest swell with pride; he practically strutted up to the lane to take his turn.

The hour passed quickly, and it seemed they'd just gotten there when Grace, David and Susanna climbed in John's truck for the ride to Pizza Palace. There, they were shown to a private room. The owner was another member of John's church, and he had provided the refreshments for the group without charge.

John found a chair next to Grace, and soon they were talking as easily as they had on the afternoons when he drove her home from the clinic. It was just comfortable between them, so easy.

"This was really nice of you," she said as she handed Susanna a straw. "They both had a fantastic time."

"They are invited again next month, if their mothers approve," he said. "And you and Dakota, of course," he added.

"Thank you."

She smiled at him, and his pulse quickened. Grace had tucked her hair up into a knot and covered it with a small prayer cap, much like the ones Leslie and Caroline wore. Grace's dress was green with a white collar and tiny buttons at the throat. He thought she was the most beautiful woman he'd ever seen. Her nose was freckled and tilted up, her face was heart-shaped and she had eyes that sparkled when she looked at him.

She knew he was staring at her, and she blushed prettily and looked away. "Does your church do other things like this?" she said, glancing at the group's guests, eagerly devouring the cheese pizza.

"Plenty," he admitted. "They hold fundraisers to help educate two children in Peru, assist in housing repairs for the elderly locally — I volunteer for that. I put my way through college working at construction, so it's something I'm comfortable doing. And I know Leslie and Kyle help with the local Meals on Wheels program.

"Next Saturday is a Christmas bazaar," John said, "but that's to benefit the Mennonite School."

"You have your own school?"

He nodded. "Some of our members send their kids to public schools, but the majority educate their children privately. The bazaar is great. It gets bigger every year. I'd love to take you and Dakota, if you'd like to come. And Susanna and David, if you think they'd enjoy it. There's food and entertainment. They show movies for the kids that even Bishop Atlee would approve of, and we have our own popcorn machine."

"It sounds like fun. Dakota would love it. I'm not making any promises, but I'll mention it to Hannah and my sisters."

He smiled at her, and a delicious warmth curled in her chest. How easy it would be to let herself fall for John. *If only* . . . Grace caught herself. Why couldn't he have been Amish? Then all her problems would have been solved.

"You know you're always welcome at our church services, Grace. I know that you attend the Amish ones, but we worship every Sunday. I'd like you to come with me."

"A Mennonite service?" She shook her head. "It's not what I want, John. I don't know how to make you understand. I want to be . . . I have to be Amish."

"Maybe, but it wouldn't hurt to make certain. Ours is a solid faith. It's given me more than I could ever put into words. Don't forget, your sister Leah chose our path. It's not that far from the Old Amish way."

She shook her head. She could feel tears stinging the back of her eyelids, but she wouldn't let them fall. "No," she said quietly. "It's not what God wants for me."

"Are you certain of that?" John asked. "Or are you just too stubborn to see what's right in front of you?"

CHAPTER TWELVE

Grace, Susanna and David returned to the Yoder house to find the kitchen crowded. After removing their outer garments and hanging them by the door, Susanna hurried to Hannah and began to tell her about the bowling, while a grinning David found his mother. In his hurry to seek her out, he'd forgotten to take off his hat. Sadie whispered in his ear, and he cheerfully returned to the door to hang his hat on the rack with those of the other men and boys. His crown was only a little flattened but still intact. Hanging on to it so that it wouldn't fall off, he went back and squeezed into a seat between his mother and Susanna.

With a squeal of happiness, Dakota ran to Grace and jumped into her arms. She would have liked nothing more than to take him to her peaceful room, close the door and spend the evening reading to him. She didn't want to answer questions in front of strangers about the bowling and pizza, and she didn't want to talk to anyone about John Hartman bringing her home in his wagon. But Grace knew that an evening of solitude with her son was impossible.

This was a visiting Sunday, and Hannah had company: Lemuel Bontrager and five of his eight children. The Bontragers had been invited to take a light supper, and Grace's sisters were busy bringing salads, bread, vegetable soup and all manner of side dishes, cakes and pies to the table. Lemuel, a bearded bear of a man with shaggy salt-and-pepper hair ringing a shiny bald spot on the crown of his head, was seated at the head of the table. His four oversize teenage sons — Clarence, Dieter, Claas and Ernst — lined up on the back bench beside Irwin. The fifth Bontrager offspring, a thin, pinch-faced young woman that Grace judged to be somewhere between seventeen and twenty, sat between Sadie and Aunt Jezzy. Violet Bontrager noisily slurped coffee and complained of what she perceived as loose behavior of the boys and girls who'd attended last night's husking frolic at the Beachy farm. She talked nonstop in a nasally whine, all the while staring at Grace with a disapproving glare. She paid no heed to the dribbles of coffee dripping from the corners of her mouth onto the table.

Grace gave Dakota another hug and seated him on a booster seat beside Jonah. After washing her hands at the sink and greeting the visitors, she began to help Johanna and Rebecca serve the food. Someone had set up a second table so that the Yoders, Bontragers and Kings could all sit together for their meal.

As she placed a bowl of chicken corn chowder in front of Violet, Grace smiled, murmured her own name and said that she was glad to meet her.

Violet sniffed and turned a cold shoulder before continuing her gripe to Sadie on the subject of worldly barn frolics in a respectable Amish community, most especially those including *Englishers.* "When we lived in Kentucky, we had no truck with the English, and our bishop forbade all clapping games as inappropriate. Would you believe I saw a young woman wearing a fancy dress with flowers on it? She's the one who went off with the Englisher."

Johanna plunked down a yellow crockery bowl of pickled eggs and red beets with such force that it rattled Violet's silverware. "That would be our Grace, and Grace is family," she said, "not an outsider. My sister Grace is *rumspringa.* She may dress as she pleases and she did *not* go alone with the Englisher. Our sister was with her."

Violet's long face flushed and she uttered, "Hmmph. *Rumspringa?* Long in the tooth for *rumspringa,* if you ask me."

Grace knew "long in the tooth" was a reference to an aging horse. What a charming person. Grace's fingers itched to splash the next bowl of soup over Violet's wrinkled *Kapp.* Charity, Grace reminded herself. As rude as Violet was, she was a guest in Hannah's home, and Grace would have to be polite. Maybe she could just drop a bowl of baked beans in her lap.

But Violet wasn't finished sharing her opinion. "I suppose if Grace is *rumspringa,* she's the one who brought the radio to the bonfire and played cowboy music."

"Radio?" Lemuel tugged at his scraggly beard. "Bishop Atlee allows radios?" One thick brow arched in shocked disapproval.

"Ne!" Susanna popped out of her chair and waved her soup spoon at him. "Not Grace. Erb! Erb Stutzman bringed it. Charley took the radio away."

Hannah motioned Susanna back into her seat, and David whispered something to Susanna.

"Erb was mean to King David, too!" Susanna added. "He laughed." Her eyes narrowed. "Not a good laugh. Mean."

"Mean," David echoed.

"I'm glad you would never be mean to anyone, David," his mother soothed. "Erb Stutzman should know better."

"You see, Lemuel?" Hannah passed a plate of corn muffins. "Our Charley confiscated the radio. We are not so loose as to allow our young people to listen to music."

Lemuel grunted and reached for a muffin. He waded through two bowls of soup, several chicken quarters and a mountain of German potato salad before asking Hannah how many quarts of honey Johanna harvested from her beehives the previous spring, the number of quilts she had completed in the past year and how much livestock she owned.

Rebecca rolled her eyes, gathered Katie, Jonah and Dakota and shepherded them off to bed. The rest of the visit passed much as Grace feared it would. After the Yoder women cleared the meal away, they all retired to the parlor where Violet continued her recitation of complaints; the four Bontrager boys stared at the floor, and Lemuel's conversation was confined to inquiring as to the state of Johanna's and Rebecca's health, their ages and how many acres Hannah intended to deed to them when they married.

It was quarter past nine when the Bontrager buggy pulled away from the barn. Grace went to kiss Dakota good-night again, and finding her room empty, went upstairs where she met Rebecca in the hallway.

"The three little ones are all sleeping soundly in Jonah's bed," Rebecca said. "Let him stay there. He'll be fine." She glanced down the wide steps. "Are they gone?" And when Grace assured her that they were, Rebecca grabbed her hand and pulled her into the room she and Johanna shared.

"The martyrs preserve us," Johanna said, waving Grace to one of the double beds. "Sit, sit." She pushed the door shut. "I thought Lemuel was going to ask to see my teeth."

Rebecca giggled.

"What awful people," Grace said. "Who would want to marry one of Lemuel's sons? They never said a word all night. David had more to contribute to the conversation."

"Not the sons," Rebecca said between bursts of amusement. "Lemuel is considering Johanna for his wife, his third."

"He has two more?" Grace asked, confused.

This time it was Johanna who began to chuckle. "*Ne*. He is a widower, twice over, poor man. And he isn't awful. He's a perfectly respectable suitor, if I was looking to marry again."

"Aren't you?" Grace asked. This laughing side of Johanna was one she'd rarely seen. She remembered that Johanna had defended her to Violet, and that she'd been pleasant to her the past few days. But she'd never been in Johanna's room before, and she still felt a little uncomfortable.

Trying not to be obvious, Grace glanced around the kerosene lamp-lit room, taking in the serene white walls, the simple white muslin window covering and the bare hardwood floor. There were two beds, two identical dressers and a wash stand with an antique bowl and pitcher. Between the windows stood a blanket chest, and in one corner rested an old quilt stand with an unfinished quilt hanging on it. "That's lovely," she said.

"Star of Bethlehem," Johanna said, clearly pleased. "An English woman ordered it for her daughter's wedding in July."

"All hand work," Rebecca explained. "No machine stitches."

"Your quilts are beautiful," Grace said. "You're a real artist. I don't know how you find the time to make them."

"It's hard some days," Johanna admitted. "And I'm still learning. I just do the old patterns." She kicked off her shoes and sat on the bed, curling her legs under her. "You should know, Grace, that Lemuel and his sons are not bad. They are very respectable people. Good catches, especially Lemuel."

"Lemuel?" Grace grimaced, trying hard not to imagine facing that beard across the breakfast table every morning. "You aren't considering him, are you?"

Johanna shook her head. "*Ne.* I had one husband, and I have no wish to have another." She sighed. "Lemuel has a fine farm and a good herd of milk cows, but Lemuel and I would not suit each other." She smiled. "Either of the oldest sons would make a decent match for Rebecca, though."

"Not me," Rebecca protested, holding up both hands. "I'm too young to get married. I want to have fun for a few more years. No husband and babies until I'm at least twenty-five."

Grace looked from one to the other. "How could your mother let Lemuel ask such personal questions? It was rude. The Bontragers were all rude, especially Violet."

Johanna nodded. "She was, wasn't she? But marrying Lemuel or one of the sons would not be marrying Violet. She will marry and move to her own home. Maybe you should consider Lemuel, Grace. You want to marry Amish, don't you?"

"Yes, but not . . . not someone as . . ." She struggled to find a way to put it that wouldn't sound insulting. "As old as he is."

"You're certainly too old for any of the Bontrager sons," Rebecca put in. "The oldest is Clarence." She pursed her lips. "Or is it Claas? I don't know, I can't keep them straight. Anyway, the eldest is only twenty. He still owes his father another year of work on the farm."

Grace grimaced as she remembered Clarence's long face and the uneven sprigs of sprouting whiskers on his clean-shaven chin. "Definitely too young for me. I need someone who can provide well for my son and be a good father."

"Lemuel could, but he won't consider you," Johanna pronounced. "Not until you join the church and remain faithful for years."

"And learn proper Pennsylvania Dutch," Rebecca said.

"That, too," Johanna agreed. "You are older than me *and* English."

"I'm *not* English," Grace protested. "I was only raised among them. And Bishop Atlee

204

said he would be pleased to accept me into the faith." *He hadn't said that in so many words,* Grace thought, *but it was certainly what he'd meant.* "There's no rule to keep me from joining the church."

"Few, if any, outsiders succeed," Johanna reminded her. "Our rules are strict. Had your mother remained with her family, she and Dat would have married, made confession, repented of their mistake and been accepted back into the fold."

"People would have forgiven them?" It was a question Grace had asked herself many times.

"We must," Johanna assured her. "If we can't forgive those who repent, how can we expect the Lord to forgive us?"

"Can He forgive anything?" Grace asked. "Could you?"

Johanna sighed. "For me, forgiving comes hard. My Wilmer . . . he took his own life. I know that I should forgive him. It's something I pray about every day. I can pray for his soul, for him as my children's father, but forgiving him is difficult."

"Your mother told me what happened." Grace traced the pattern of a blue heart on the quilt beneath them. "I'm sorry. It must have been terrible for you and the children."

"My Wilmer was a troubled man. Sick in

spirit. In some ways, it will be easier for Jonah and Katie without him. Me . . ." A shadow passed across Johanna's face. "Sometimes, I go for hours now without thinking of him."

Grace's insides clenched. It was the same with Joe, except sometimes it was days before she thought of him. How strange it was that she and Johanna's lives were so similar.

Johanna smoothed wrinkles from her apron and looked up. "But if you do stay with us, Grace, you will have to find a husband. And having men come to the house and ask about you is how it's done." She sighed. "And the truth is, it will only be an older widower who would consider you. Maybe even a man much older than Lemuel."

Rebecca nodded. "Or one with nine or ten children to cook and sew for. Could you do that?"

An uneasy feeling curled in the pit of Grace's stomach. "Anna did. Not nine children, but five. Look how happy she and Samuel are."

"Samuel and Anna." Johanna chuckled. "Who would have thought it?"

"She's still the talk of three states," Rebecca said. "Don't expect another Samuel

Mast to drop out of an apple tree."

Johanna pressed warm fingers against Grace's wrist. "And you aren't Anna, Grace. Even for her, it's hard to manage so large a household, especially with the new baby coming."

"But having a man look me over like that, like tonight . . ." Grace said. "I don't know. Don't you find it insulting?"

Rebecca shrugged. "It's the way it's done."

"For Rebecca, who is young and attractive and never married, it will be easier to find a husband," Johanna explained. "While you and I, should I ever want to marry again, must be content to wait for some middle-aged widower to come knocking at Mam's door."

"Are you telling me that the women don't get to choose?" Grace asked.

Johanna considered the question before answering. "We do choose, but we depend on family and community to help in that choice. And we must find a husband from who's available. First, you would want a devout man, a faithful member of the church. And then, as you say, one who would be a good provider."

"Kind," Rebecca put in. "Hopefully, even-tempered."

"Which is why Lemuel Bontrager would

not be a bad match for you, Grace. If he would have you — which he won't. By the time you are ready to marry Amish, some other woman will have snapped him up."

"Even with Violet to contend with?" Grace teased.

"*Ya,*" Johanna replied. "Even with Violet and the seven boys." She chuckled. "So, big sister . . ." Her eyes twinkled. "Don't be so quick to turn away John Hartman."

"John?" Grace felt her throat and face grow warm. "He isn't Amish."

"Neither are you," Rebecca pointed out.

"You don't understand," Grace argued. "I can't consider John. Marrying Amish is something I have to do. I couldn't stand to lose all of you now that I've come to love you."

Johanna stood up. "I suppose you know your own mind better than we do. But . . ." She hesitated. "As our father always told me, 'Open your eyes, Johanna. Sometimes the thing that will make you happiest is right in front of your face and you're just too stubborn to see it.' "

On Thursday evening, John arrived home in time to share a hot meal with his grandfather and uncle. He'd had another crazy week, and the only time he'd been able to speak to Grace had been a few minutes two days earlier when she had finished work and was waiting for the van to pick her up. He'd offered to drive her home, but she'd refused. Shamelessly, he'd reminded her of the Christmas bazaar on Saturday and had invited her to a potluck supper his church was having afterward. Grace hadn't refused, but she hadn't accepted, either, and he couldn't help wondering if she was still put out with him over the whole hay wagon episode.

"You're just in time," Gramps said as John entered the kitchen. "You're in for a real treat."

John glanced at Uncle Albert and groaned. "What is it? Fish sticks and canned peas again? Or that frozen lasagna that tastes like cardboard with ketchup poured over it?"

"You'll be laughing out of the other side of your face once you taste my one-dish wonder," Gramps said. Uncle Albert made a show of trying to lift the lid off the Crock-Pot and peek inside. "No, you don't," Gramps said, smacking Uncle Albert's fingers with a long-handled wooden spoon. "And it's your turn to wash dishes, Albert."

"It's not," John's uncle protested. "It's John's turn. I washed last night."

John laughed as he retrieved napkins from

the counter. "No, you didn't. If you recall, you had that emergency. You had to check the IV pump on Bruce Taylor's poodle. At eight o'clock at night." The animal hospital was right next door, but it was amazing how long it could take his uncle to check on a patient when there were dishes to be washed.

"Never can tell," Uncle Albert replied. "That pump might not have been running properly and then Elvis would have been in dire straits."

"Convenient timing," Gramps grumbled. "Getting you to load the dishwasher is like trying to get a cat to clean its own litter box. Mighty rare occurrence."

Everyone laughed and then the three gathered around the table, sat and held hands while Gramps asked the blessing. He then carried the Crock-Pot to the table. "Behold," he said, whipping off the glass lid. "My masterpiece."

"It's Hamburger Helper with that funny-shaped rice, isn't it?" John teased.

"Be thankful for what you receive," Gramps said. "People in third-world countries would consider this a feast." He scooped out a congealed lump of mystery supper and dropped it onto John's plate.

"I was right," John said, reaching for the

hot sauce. "Burger and a box of dried mystery ingredients."

"With peas and canned corn added," Gramps said proudly. "Smells delicious, doesn't it?"

"Smells like a barn that needs to be cleaned," Uncle Albert observed. "Are you sure you didn't add hoof trimmings to this?" He stuck a fork into his portion and left it standing upright. "How many hours did you leave this in the Crock-Pot, Dad?"

"Nine, ten tops."

Gramps sat down in front of his portion, took a forkful and chewed slowly. John and his uncle watched as Gramps washed the first bite down with water, liberally salted the meat, rice and vegetable mix and took another bite. Then, he dropped the fork and began to laugh deep belly laughs. Uncle Albert and John joined in, laughing until tears rolled down their cheeks.

"A masterpiece," Uncle Albert proclaimed between guffaws.

Gramps shook his head, then looked at John. "Well, boy, are you going to call for pizza delivery or am I?" And then they all laughed again.

Uncle Albert pulled his cell phone from his shirt pocket and hit the speed dial. "Albert Hartman," he said. "Yes, the usual.

Thanks a lot." He closed the phone. "Twenty minutes." He looked down at the plates. "I suppose we could save this for —"

John shook his head. "Not even the Yoders' chickens could eat this."

"Guess not." Gramps was still chuckling. "But while we're waiting for that pizza delivery, Albert and I want to talk to you about something. It concerns Grace Yoder."

John's stomach clenched. Grace was one subject he didn't want to talk about. "Business or personal?"

"The practice," Uncle Albert said.

John almost heaved a sigh of relief. "Grace is doing her job, isn't she?"

"Absolutely." Uncle Albert gathered up the plates and scraped the inedible meal into the trash can. "Sue came to me this morning. It seems Grace is a wonder. Not only is she the best kennel tech we've ever had working for us, but she's very observant. She picked up on a case of diabetes in the Winklers' cat. It was just here for boarding while the Winklers went on vacation. Sue says Grace is a natural with animals."

"I'm glad she's working out," John said, wondering where this was heading.

"You know Patel's practice at the beach — the big one? Sue says that they're sending a young woman to Del Tech for their vet tech program. It's not a bad idea for us to consider doing the same. You know how difficult it is to find and keep good techs."

"I know," John agreed. "And as happy as Melody seems here, and as much as we like her, her husband's Air Force. He could get orders and we'd lose her."

"What would you think if we offered Grace Yoder a scholarship?" His uncle rinsed off the plates. "We could work out something where she could stay on, at least part-time while she went to school. But it's a big commitment. Do you believe she'd be interested?"

"I don't know," John answered slowly. "I think she'd make a great vet tech, but she doesn't have a car. We'd have to come up with transportation for her, so she could get back and forth to school." He was so relieved that neither of them had brought up his personal relationship with Grace that he was babbling. "Maybe we could —"

"That's no problem," Gramps interrupted. "Your grandmother's Buick is sitting in the garage. Hasn't been started since she passed, but it's in good shape. Not more than 50,000 miles on it. The girl may as well drive it as have it rust away. I should have sold it three years ago, but there's a lot of things I should do. Grace has a little boy to support, doesn't she?"

John nodded. "He's three years old."

"Well, you tell her to come and speak to me. It's not easy for a woman to raise a child alone. If she's willing to work for us for what we pay, I think I can let her have that car, whether she wants to study to be a vet tech or not. It's a solid vehicle, be safe for the child."

"That's good of you, Gramps." John fiddled with his napkin. "But I have to tell you that Grace thinks she wants to become Amish. She may not accept the car."

Uncle Albert smiled and shook his head. "That's not going to happen. The only person I ever knew around here who joined the Amish from the outside is Hannah Yoder. And the Old Order Mennonite church she was raised in wasn't much different. I don't think we have to worry about Grace giving up the world."

"So you think it's a good idea?" Gramps asked.

"I do," John agreed. He hoped Grace would accept.

"Need to talk to you about something else, too," his grandfather said, "while we're at it."

By the time John realized where his grandfather was headed, it was too late to make a hasty retreat.

"This relationship you have with this girl. She's an employee, John. Business and friendship don't always make for good partners."

"I've thought about that," he replied, "but I think it's too late. If you want the truth, I think I'm already in love with her."

"You thought you were in love with Miriam Yoder," Uncle Albert pointed out good-naturedly. "What is it with you and those Yoder girls?"

"I thought I was at the time," John admitted. "But this is different — the way I feel about Grace is different. I'm scared. I got my heart broken before with Miriam, and I know I'm taking a big chance. If it happens again with Grace, it will be a lot worse." He looked first into his uncle's face and then met his grandfather's level gaze. "I want to marry Grace, and I want to be a father to her son."

"Sounds to me like you've thought this through pretty good," Gramps said. "Prayed over it, have you?"

"Every night," John said.

"Then you've got to take the chance," Uncle Albert said. "You can't go through life afraid. Sometimes, you have to take a leap of faith and hope for the best."

CHAPTER THIRTEEN

Grace gave in and went to the bazaar at the Mennonite School with John. Once there, she was glad she had. It was the kind of Christmas atmosphere that she dreamed of but knew she wouldn't find in the Yoder household. Both she and Dakota enjoyed it tremendously. Familiar carols filled the air as the three of them drank hot chocolate and stopped to admire an elaborate model train display featuring a snow-covered papier-mâché mountain, miniature farms and a Victorian village.

Grace, John and Dakota wandered up and down the aisles of craft tables, tasting samples of brownies and Christmas goodies and chatting with John's friends and clients. Grace was pleasantly surprised to see that many of the shoppers were Amish. She wished Susanna could have come with her, but her sister had decided at the last minute to accompany Rebecca to Anna's to bake cookies. Grace suspected her choice had more to do with the possibility of David's presence there than her desire to bake, but Grace's feelings weren't hurt. In a way, she was proud of the stubbornness Susanna was displaying in regard to her friendship with David.

After walking around for a while, John had to excuse himself to act as short-order cook in the kitchen while a friend took a lunch break. "Not the best choice," John remarked as he donned an apron. "I'm not much of a cook." He flashed a smile at her. "Hopefully, I can manage hot dogs and hamburgers."

"We need him for only an hour," a rosy-cheeked, middle-aged woman with a lace prayer cap called through the open kitchen door. She waved to Grace.

Grace waved back and led Dakota away. She'd drawn Jonah's name in the family gift exchange, and had planned to take this time to search for a special present for him. As with all else, as Rebecca had considerately explained, Amish Christmases were austere and noncommercial. Jonah would receive a few simple items from Johanna, including a new pair of boots, mittens and a toolbox with a small hammer and screwdriver. Other than those, the gift Grace purchased would be all he received.

Christmas fell on a church Sunday this year, but Hannah had explained to Grace that services would be postponed until the following week. December twenty-fifth would be a quiet family day of prayer, fasting and Bible reading. The following day was the Amish Second Christmas, the time for visiting and gift giving. Hannah and the girls would prepare a big holiday dinner for the occasion.

Grace led Dakota around a table and his eyes grew wide and he bounced up and down at the sight of a big Christmas tree. The decorations were all handmade, and instead of lights, someone had strung popcorn and cranberries to adorn the boughs. Beneath the tree, visitors to the bazaar and members of the Mennonite Church had left heaps of wrapped gifts designated for local children of incarcerated parents. "Look! Look, Mommy!" Dakota cried. "Are we having a Christmas tree?"

Grace's heart sank. "No," she said softly. "The Amish don't believe in them." She bent and hugged her son. "But this year, we'll be with family. It will be a wonderful Christmas, I promise you."

They strolled on, lingering near a small stage where a high-school student played

"Oh, Little Town of Bethlehem" on a much-loved and battered piano, accompanied by a young man with a guitar. The sweet notes brought tears to Grace's eyes, and she squeezed Dakota's hand tighter. *We're not giving up Christmas,* she told herself. *We're just moving to a simpler celebration of Christ's birth.*

Still, she stood transfixed, listening to the music, unable to keep her thoughts from drifting. A long, long time ago . . . That year, the highlight of the holiday for her had been the opportunity to play the part of the innkeeper's wife in a Sunday-school pageant. There had been a small pile of gifts for her under her foster mother's tree, but she couldn't remember a single one. What she did remember was the excitement of standing behind the dusty drapes waiting to step on stage and recite her lines.

It had been a bitter night with a foot of snow on the ground and wind that howled around the corners of the building. It was so cold that each breath Grace took sent little clouds of condensation into the air. But when those first notes of "Oh, Little Town of Bethlehem" wheezed from the church organ, she'd been transfixed by the magic and beauty of Christmas.

The Christmas pageant was one of

Grace's most treasured memories, one that had given her pleasure over the years. Secretly, she had always hoped that Dakota would get to experience that same thrill some day. He might even get to play the part of Joseph or one of the three kings when he was older. She smiled at her own foolishness. What she was giving him was far more important: a family, a sense of community and a faith to sustain him when life got tough. . . . Because it would. Grace wasn't naive enough to think that becoming Amish would solve *all* their problems. Being Amish didn't mean that bad things would never happen to her or Dakota. It simply meant that if they did, she and he would be able to accept God's will and find the strength to carry on.

"I want a guitar," Dakota said. "I want to play a guitar like you."

Grace swallowed, trying to ignore the inner twinge of regret that thoughts of her beloved guitar brought to mind. Musical instruments were forbidden to the Amish, and she'd stored her guitar in Hannah's attic. *I should sell it or give it away,* she thought. *The longer I hold on to it, the more difficult it will be to let it go. Someone may as well enjoy it.*

"Come on," she said, hurrying Dakota

away. "We have to find a gift for Jonah. Remember? But it's a surprise. You can't tell what we get him."

"I won't tell," he promised, glancing back over his shoulder at the guitar player as she tugged him away.

"We need something special." Grace glanced around at the booths containing gently used items. "Something that doesn't need batteries."

"Look!" Dakota pointed. Under a table, sticking out of a cardboard box, was a red roof. "It's a barn," he said. "Like one at my old school."

Grace knelt to pull out the box. Inside was a sturdy plastic barn filled with a tumbled heap of matching animals: cows, horses, chickens, a goat and pigs. There were sections of fence and even a tiny milk bucket and toy bales of hay. "I hope it's not too expensive," she murmured. The toys were well-made and perfect for a small Amish boy, but Johanna had warned her not to spend more than twenty dollars.

The gray-haired lady behind the counter smiled at Dakota when Grace asked how much the barn set was. "For you, young man?" the woman asked Dakota.

He shook his head. "For my cousin. For Christmas." He brought his finger to his lips. "But it's a secret," he warned in a loud whisper.

The woman lifted the box onto the table and examined the barn. "It isn't new," she said. "And one of the doors is cracked on the barn, and there's a little water stain inside. Wait." She rummaged behind the counter and came up with a tiny wagon and a handful of toy sheep. "This must go with it. I've been wondering what to do with those sheep. Would ten dollars be too much?"

"Not at all." Grace was counting out the money when Leslie, whom she'd met at the bowling outing the previous Saturday, approached her. Three small children trailed her.

Grace thanked the woman at the table and turned away, the box with the barn and animals in her arms.

"Hi," Leslie said. "John sent me to look for you. We're starting a movie about the nativity story in the auditorium and he thought Dakota might enjoy it. We're going to have popcorn and apple juice. If you'll let me take him, I'll watch out for him. I promise."

"Can I?" Dakota looked up at Grace with a sweet smile on his face. "Can I go?"

"It's just right through that doorway," Leslie explained. "You can join us, too, if you like."

"All right," Grace agreed. "I just want to get the truck keys from John and put this —" she lifted the box "— into the cab."

Dakota waved as he walked away, holding Leslie's hand.

By the time Grace reached the cafeteria window, John was already finishing his shift. He insisted on carrying Jonah's present to the truck. "I've wanted to get you alone all morning," he said. "I have something important to talk to you about."

"What is it?" Grace asked, fighting an uneasy feeling. She hoped John didn't want to talk about dating again. He was wearing her down with his kindness.

"It's about work." He smiled at her. "Wait until we get outside."

Relieved and intrigued, Grace followed him to the truck. John slid the box of toys onto the backseat, and then opened the passenger front door for her to get in. "It's too cold to stand out here." He went around to the driver's side and joined her in the cab. "Uncle Albert and my grandfather came up with this idea," he said. "It's a great opportunity. I hope you'll at least think about it."

Grace listened as John explained about

223

the vet tech associate's degree the community college offered. A small flame of hope flared in the pit of her stomach. She tamped it down. She couldn't be understanding this correctly. The Hartmans couldn't possibly be offering to send her to college — to pay for her to learn a profession. She loved working with animals, but she'd never imagined that she'd ever have the chance to. . . .

"They believe in you," John continued. "I believe in you. We think that you can do this."

He went on to tell her the solutions they'd come up with for continued part-time work at the clinic and transportation, but she was still stunned by the possibilities. Being a vet tech would mean more money and a real career. She was speechless.

"So what do you think?" John clasped her hand in his. "Is it something that you'd consider?"

She swallowed, trying to dissolve the lump in her throat, and then burst into tears. Mortified, she jerked her hand away and covered her face, unable to hold back.

"Grace, don't," he begged. "Don't cry. What did I say?" He reached for her and she buried her face in his coat and sobbed.

"Did I say something wrong? Did I insult you?"

She pulled back, now beginning to laugh through the tears. "No," she managed. "I'm . . . I'm . . . just . . . so happy." She wanted to turn handstands in the parking lot. She shook her head, wanting to pinch herself to be certain this wasn't a dream. She fumbled in her purse for a tissue but couldn't find one.

He pulled a clean red-and-white handkerchief from his coat pocket and handed it to her. "If you're happy, you have a weird way of showing it."

She chuckled and he began to laugh with her as she wiped her eyes and blew her nose on the handkerchief. "I don't know what to say," she gasped. "I feel like such an idiot."

"But you're pleased?"

She nodded. "Thrilled."

"Great. Fantastic."

She balled the handkerchief and stuck it in her own coat pocket. "I can't believe it. I never thought I'd ever have the chance to go to college. I always wanted to, but . . ." Her eyes filled with tears again.

"So you'd do it?" he insisted, rubbing her arm. "You're willing to do it?"

"Yes, yes, of course." She looked into his eyes and began to laugh again. "What kind of man carries handkerchiefs in his pocket?"

John groaned. "I know. I know. But Uncle Albert always does, and my aunt kept putting them in my pocket when I was a boy. I guess it's a habit."

"That came in handy today," Grace admitted.

"It did, didn't it?" John's smile widened and she couldn't help thinking how handsome he was.

"So you'll do it?"

"I . . ." She hesitated, suddenly struck by the thought that it might not be entirely up to her. "Unless . . ." Her stomach pitched. "Unless it's against the rules . . . Amish rules. I don't suppose being a vet tech is much different than what I'm doing now," she said hopefully. "But I'll have to ask . . . ask Hannah."

"You have time. The next session doesn't begin until February."

"I'll talk to her first thing when I get home."

"You and Dakota are still staying for the potluck supper, aren't you? The kids have a great time." He looked into her eyes. "I want you to, Grace. Please say you'll stay."

Moth wings fluttered in the pit of her stomach. She opened the truck door and sucked in a deep breath of cold, fresh air.

When she summoned nerve enough to look back at him, she was struck by the vulnerability in his face. "Are you certain I . . . we'll be welcome?"

She was stalling, wanting to refuse, wanting to keep this as a day between friends . . . not a date. Letting herself care about John was dangerous. She couldn't have both John and the forgiveness she needed to go forward with her life. No matter how she wished that things could be different, John couldn't fit into her plan.

"Of course you'd both be welcome, but . . ." He knotted his right hand, pressing it against the leather seat. "I don't want to pressure you, Grace. I don't want you to feel uncomfortable. But I think you know that I'd like us to be more than friends."

She nodded. "It's probably best if you take us home. So that I can talk to Hannah," she added quickly. "This . . . the bazaar has been great. I've had a good time . . . really. But . . ."

He nodded. "All right. I understand."

But you don't, she thought, reading the disappointment in his eyes. *You don't understand at all. And if you knew the truth about me, you probably wouldn't want to have anything to do with me again. Ever.*

■ ■ ■ ■

Two hours later, Grace stood in Hannah's kitchen staring at her stepmother in bewilderment. "I don't understand," Grace said. "I'll have to work part-time for two years until I finish the program, but I'll still be bringing money into the house. And after that, when I've become a vet tech, my wages will —"

"Ne," Hannah repeated. She laid the rolling pin on the floured board and folded her arms over her chest and shook her head. "I am sorry, Grace, but you cannot do this."

"Is it because of the driving? I could take a van to school if you don't want me to use the car." She hadn't known about this opportunity a few hours ago, and now she wanted it desperately.

"Oh, child." Hannah's expression softened and she dusted her floury hands on her apron. "You can't do this at all."

"But why?" Grace's chest tightened.

"If you truly want to be one of us, you must learn to accept the rules of our community. We do not believe in higher education. It's why our children don't go to high school or to any English school at all. It's why they leave the classroom after the eighth grade. There is no college for us," she added softly.

"But it doesn't make any sense," Grace argued.

Hannah took several steps and extended a hand. "I told you that it wouldn't be easy . . . for you to make the journey from your world into ours. You must understand."

"Maybe if I went to the elders and explained . . ."

Again Hannah shook her head. "You heard what the bishop told you. He will make no decisions for you. But if you do this, you will not be allowed to become one of us." She offered a half smile. "Believe me, daughter, no Amish man would consider you as wife if you persist."

"But you work," Grace argued. "You're a teacher. Surely —"

"I had worked as a teacher before I married and returned to it after Jonas died. I did have some studies by mail, but I never went to college. And if . . . *when* I remarry, I won't be allowed to work any longer."

"How can a higher education interfere with my becoming Amish? With how I serve God?"

"Some things must not be questioned, but simply accepted. Remember, we are a people commanded to remain apart from the world. If you want to continue, you must refuse this offer and keep cleaning the kennels or find another job . . . a job suitable for an Amish woman. You must do this if you want to be considered for admittance to the church."

"There's no way?"

"None," Hannah replied. "You must choose, Grace. This college or our faith."

She nodded. *She wouldn't cry, she couldn't.* She felt numb inside. *This means that Dakota can never attend college, either,* she realized. *Not even high school.* Slowly, she lowered her head in defeat.

"Your choice," Hannah repeated. "You must learn to accept the *Ordnung,* to submit your will to the laws of our community. Or find a different path," she said softly.

"I have to tell John," she said. "He's waiting outside in the truck. It's only fair. That way, they can find someone else."

"I'm sorry," Hannah said. "I know this seems unfair to you, but it's best. And if you've made up your mind, best to let him know your decision."

Woodenly, Grace left the kitchen, not even stopping long enough to put on her coat. She didn't feel the cold as she crossed the porch and passed through the open gate. John saw her, smiled and waved. She straightened her shoulders, knowing that explaining why she couldn't accept his offer would be hard.

He got out of the truck and came toward her. "What did Hannah say?" he called. "Does she think the bishop will allow —"

She raised a hand, palm up, and a gust of wind hit her hard enough to almost knock her off her feet. "It isn't what you wanted to hear," she said, raising her voice. "I'm sorry, but . . ." She stumbled through the explanation, repeating the phrases Hannah had used. How could she expect him to understand when he didn't know her reasons?

"No! You can't let them dictate to you, Grace. This is too important a decision for anyone else to make for you. You want it. I know you do."

"I can't fight this," she said, wrapping her arms around her waist. "If I went to college, I couldn't join the church."

"Then don't join the church. Have the courage to make your own life. You have a God-given talent for working with sick and hurt animals. It would be a sin to waste that gift because . . ."

He was upset, more than upset. John was angry with her. Suddenly weary and heartsick, she stopped listening to him. It wasn't just the job. John still hadn't realized that

231

there was no future for them.

"Stop!" she said. "Just stop talking and listen to me." She tried to sound tough, but her teeth were chattering. It was difficult to be forceful when she was so cold that goose bumps were rising on her arms and legs. "I need to tell you something . . . something that will . . ."

"You're shivering," he said, removing his fleece-lined jean jacket and draping it around her shoulders. "Get in the truck."

"Is that an order?"

"*Please* get in the truck."

What difference did it make? Once he knew what she was, she probably wouldn't even have her kennel tech position. But it didn't matter. She was tired of living a lie . . . tired of hiding.

She was still shivering after she climbed inside the cab. She pulled John's coat around her, raised her chin and looked him in the eye. *God help me,* she prayed. *I have to tell him.*

"Okay," he said, putting his arm on the back of the seat. "Let's have it. You're still married to Dakota's father, aren't you? You're going to tell me that I've fallen hard for a married woman."

"That's just it," she whispered huskily. She

232

made herself look him in the eyes. "There is no husband. There never was."

CHAPTER FOURTEEN

John waited. Grace stared down at her hands . . . small hands, unpolished, but strong and graceful. Like she was, he thought. He loved Grace's hands . . . wanted to take them in his and hold them and never let go.

Silence stretched between them. "That's it?" he finally asked. "You weren't married when Dakota was born? That's what's making you so unhappy?"

Her answer came in a small voice, the tones almost childlike. "You know what that makes my son?" She looked him in the eyes. "What people will call him if they know?"

"Mean-spirited people. But they won't say it around me or Hannah or your sisters, I can promise you that." He reached for her hand, but she shrank away, hunching against the door, clutching his coat around her. Her shoulders trembled. *Was she crying?* The instinct to protect her that he'd felt when they'd first met rushed back, a hundred times stronger. She was so young to have faced so many obstacles so bravely. But she wasn't alone anymore, not if he could help it.

"Grace, look at me."

She pressed her face against the glass. "I haven't told anyone. Even Hannah doesn't know." A small sob shook her. "When I tell her, I'll probably have to leave."

"That's crazy. Do you think that your family would turn against you for a mistake? That *I* would?"

Her breath fogged the window and she rubbed at it with a slender fingertip. "Because I lied . . . because I let everyone believe that I was a widow."

"Dakota's father abandoned the two of you?"

"No." Her breath caught in her throat with a small sound. "He *was* a bull rider. He *was* killed in a rodeo accident."

John couldn't help feeling a little relieved that Grace hadn't lied about her husband passing away, that she didn't have an old love who could come back into her life to claim her and Dakota. He tried to tell himself that it was despicable to feel that for the passing of another human being, but all he could think of was that Grace and

Dakota — *his* Grace and Dakota were free.

Hope replaced uncertainty as his heartbeat quickened. No matter what it took, he'd convince her that she wasn't meant to be Amish. She liked riding in his truck and listening to the radio. She was friendly and outgoing with the people who came to the office, and she had a special way with animals. And no matter how hard she tried to convince him otherwise, he knew that she desperately wanted to further her education for her future and that of her son.

"Broncs, too."

John snapped out of his thoughts. Grace was speaking to him. Had he been thinking of her so intensely that he'd missed something important? "Excuse me," he said. "Broncs?"

"Bucking broncos. Rodeo horses. He rode them." She half turned. Her voice was little more than a whisper, but huskier than a little girl's. It resonated under his skin. "As I told you, Joe Eagle, Dakota's father, was Native American."

"Dakota's a beautiful child, and his heritage is something to be proud of."

"He looks different than his cousins. He always will."

"He's an individual, Grace, as are you. It's a good thing." He hesitated, and then asked the question that had troubled him the most. "Did you love him — Dakota's father?"

"I thought I did." She shivered, nearly lost in his big coat. "Yes, I did love him at first. I wanted so bad to have someone, a husband . . . a home. But Joe wasn't an easy man to live with. He had his own demons to fight, and sometimes he took it out on Dakota and me. When Joe died, I think I was more sad than grieving. Such a waste . . ." Her mouth firmed. "And when —"

"It doesn't matter," John said. "That's all in the past. You don't have to tell me anything you don't want to."

"But I want to." Some of the spunk came back into her and she raised her pointed chin and met his gaze straight on. Her blue eyes glistened with tears. "It was wrong of me to deceive Hannah and . . . and everyone. You don't know how many nights I've lain awake praying for forgiveness . . . praying for the strength to tell the truth. I did exactly what Joe did, deceived the ones I should have been the most honest with. But I was so scared . . ." A single tear welled up and splashed against a pale cheek. "We're all alone, the two of us. I wanted someone . . . somewhere to belong."

John fought the urge to pull her into his arms, to cradle her against his chest and promise to make everything all right. The desire to protect her, to make her his wife and to become a real father to Dakota was nearly overwhelming. But he could sense that like a terrified filly that had tangled herself in a barbed-wire fence, if he came on too fast or too strong, she'd panic.

Life had buffeted Grace Yoder until she was at the breaking point. If he reached for her, she might run, and he could lose any chance of making her understand that none of it mattered — that he could never judge her for the mistake of having a child out of wedlock. "Grace, it's all right," he soothed with the same tone he'd use on an injured filly.

"No! It's not. You have to listen. I don't know if I've got the nerve to tell this twice."

He nodded, folding his hands to be sure he didn't reach for her. "If you want to, but I'm here for you. Believe me, I know what kind of person you are. If you made a mistake —"

"My mistake was in being stupid. When I first met Joe, I was stranded in the middle of nowhere. I'd been walking for hours, and it was almost dark when he stopped to pick me up in his truck. They can say all they want about cowboys, but he didn't come on to me like I was cheap."

John shook his head. "No one could ever call you cheap, Grace."

"Just listen, *please,*" she begged.

John nodded and Grace went on. "Joe drove me to the next town and introduced me to a retired Baptist minister and his wife who followed the rodeo circuit. Mrs. Bray had broken her hip and needed help. I stayed with them for two months until the season was over. Joe and I dated, but I never did anything to be ashamed of, not with him, not with any man. Then Joe asked me to marry him. I was afraid that he'd leave and I'd never see him again. I knew that it was too soon, that we hadn't known each other long enough, but I said yes, anyway."

"I don't understand," John said. "He asked you to marry him, but then went back on his word?"

"Oh, he married me, all right. Reverend Bray married us and Mrs. Bray witnessed it. I have a license from the State of Wyoming to prove it."

"If you had a marriage ceremony, then . . ." His shoulders tightened. "This Bray wasn't a real minister?"

"He was the real thing, all right. It was Joe who wasn't the real thing."

"I don't understand," John protested. "How could —"

"Shh." She put her fingers over his lips. "I'm trying to tell you. After . . . after the accident, things were bad. There were so many bills. Joe had told me he was an orphan, that he didn't have anyone like me. But when I was going through his things, I found a Christmas card from his mother, dated the previous December. I wrote to the address, but I didn't get an answer. For Dakota's sake, I had to try to make some kind of connection with her. I'd had to sell Joe's truck for rent money, and it took me a long time to get enough money for another vehicle. When I did, we drove to the reservation. I just wanted her to meet her grandson."

John winced at the pain etched across her face.

"I found her, but I wish I hadn't. She called me awful names — told me she wished Dakota had never been born. She said that I'd tricked her son, led him to abandon his family — that we should be the ones dead, not Joe." A sob shook her. "You see, I thought I was Joe's wife, but I wasn't. He already had a wife and two children on the reservation. He was married to a woman named Bernadette when he made his vows to me. So . . . so, I was never really Mrs. Joe Eagle. I was just Grace Yoder."

She reached for the door latch, but John seized her arm. "It's not your fault," he said. "If there was wrong, it was Joe's, not yours, and not Dakota's. How could anyone blame you for —"

She whipped around. "For being stupid? For believing a good-looking rodeo rider with a two-thousand-dollar saddle and a mouthful of lies?" She pulled free. "It's why I have to become Amish, John. It's why I have to do this. If I accept baptism in the Amish faith, God will forgive me — the stain on Dakota's birth will be wiped away."

"Grace, listen to me!"

But it was too late. She flung open the door and jumped out. He climbed out the passenger door and followed her halfway to the gate. "Wait! Can't we talk?"

She stopped and looked back. "Your coat," she said, slipping it off and throwing it to him.

"Grace, listen, I know you're upset. I can come back later. Tomorrow —"

"No." She shook her head. "There's nothing left to say. I've made up my mind, and you won't talk me out of what I know is the right thing to do for me and my son."

"Wanting God in your life is a good thing," he said. "But your father's path isn't the only one."

"It's my business, John! Not yours. No one asked you to interfere in my life."

He felt as though a hard fist had punched him in the gut. He stood there, coat dangling in his hand with the rain pelting his face. "All right, I'm sorry you feel that way. But maybe you're right. Maybe it isn't any of my business. I'll pick you up Monday morning for work, and then we can —"

"No." She started for the house again. "I can see now that I should never have taken the job in the first place. I have to be apart from the world. Being at the clinic —"

"I won't let you quit," he said, following her through the gate. "It's not what you want — not what I want."

"You can't stop me from quitting." She was shivering again. "Tell your uncle that I'm sorry to not give notice, but it's best for everyone if I leave now without a fuss."

"You're making the biggest mistake of your life," he said. "You think about it — about what you're doing. About what's best for Dakota. I'll be here Monday morning."

"Didn't you just hear what I said?" she cried, stopping to turn around again. "I'm not coming. I'm not working for you anymore. Tell your uncle I appreciate the offer of the scholarship, but my new faith won't allow me to accept. Give it to someone else, someone who will appreciate it."

She ran up the steps and into the house, slamming the door behind her. John stood there, wondering what he could have done differently, feeling the woman he'd come to love slipping away from him. He got back into the truck, and tightened his fingers around the steering wheel, using every ounce of his will to keep from punching the dashboard.

Anger rode him as he started the engine and drove out of the yard and down the lane. Anger clouded his thoughts and made him doubt his judgment. Maybe his grandfather was right. Maybe he had fallen too quickly for Grace. Maybe he wanted her because Miriam had rejected him.

The wipers swished back and forth. He wanted to tramp down on the accelerator and put distance between him and Grace, but he didn't. A lifetime of concern for other people was too hard to shake. Instead, he did what he always did when he was confronted with overwhelming problems. He found a safe place to pull off the road, put his truck into park, lowered his head and murmured the Twenty-Third Psalm aloud. And as always, he found comfort in the old words from the St. James version of the Bible. When he was done, he sat in silence for a long time before uttering a simple prayer.

"God, it's John Hartman, again. I'd appreciate it if you could help me out here. I'm in deep water and I can't even see the shore."

When Grace reentered the kitchen, Hannah and Aunt Jezzy turned to look at her. "What were you thinking, child," Hannah said, "to run out in this weather without your coat?"

Grace murmured something and hurried past them into the hallway, but she didn't go to her bedroom. She wanted to be alone, and if she went there, Dakota — who was happily playing with Jonah and Katie — might follow her. Instead, she climbed the stairs to the second floor and then another flight to the attic.

The air was chilly up here, but one section was always kept as an extra guest bedroom. The space was whitewashed and tidy, the antique maple bed and stacks of quilts a welcoming retreat. She wrapped a blue-and-white quilt around her shoulders, removed her shoes and curled up on the bed. Two windows allowed light into the chamber, and even with the rain coming down, Grace could see well enough.

Telling John her secret hadn't worked out the way she expected. Why was it that nothing in her life ever did? He should have been disgusted, repelled by her deceit. Instead, he'd made excuses for her, blamed Joe and tried to talk her out of the only plan that made sense. Why couldn't John see that becoming Amish would cleanse her and secure her salvation? Why was he so stubborn? Why couldn't he accept her decision and her resignation without driving her to say awful things that would end their friendship? And why did he believe that she wasn't strong enough to renounce the world to save herself and her son?

John was the one who was in the wrong here. Why had he ruined such a beautiful day? Dakota had enjoyed the Christmas bazaar as much as she had. She'd loved the music, the decorations, the bustle of holiday shopping, and she'd been so happy with the barn set she'd found for Jonah.

When John had offered her the opportunity to become a vet tech, she couldn't believe her good fortune. She'd forgotten what was important. She'd hoped that she could have both worlds, the peace she'd found here among her father's family and friends, and the excitement of working at a job she loved.

John had meant well. She knew that. If things were different, having John in her life would have been . . .

No! She wouldn't think about that. John Hartman wasn't for her. All he was — all he could ever be — was a temptation. Letting herself fall in love with John would ruin everything. And she could . . . so easily . . . she could. She could imagine the three of them, John, her and Dakota, laughing together over the supper table, cutting down a Christmas tree and decorating it, singing along with the country and Christian artists on his truck radio.

She could choose John and his way of life . . . even now. She could go to him and say she was sorry, ask him if they could start over. And he would agree; she was certain of it. But in opening her heart to John and his world, she would be closing the door to what mattered most. Forgiveness.

The rainfall intensified, and big drops spattered against the windowpanes. The Lord had brought her this far. It would be wrong to abandon the plan now. Her mother and father had both been born into the Amish faith. She wasn't doing anything radical, not really. She was simply coming home, where she belonged, where she and her precious little son would find peace and happiness. If the price of that was giving up John, so be it. This was her last chance to turn her life around.

Far better to choose a good man, even one like Lemuel Bontrager, and marry him. What had Hannah said? Marriage was bigger than two people. Surely, if she picked a solid Amish husband, one she could respect, love would follow. And if it didn't, she'd married for what she thought was love once before, and that match had turned hollow.

She could never wish that she hadn't met Joe. If not for Joe, she wouldn't have Dakota, and life without her son was impossible to consider. She'd made a foolish decision when she married Joe Eagle, and she couldn't make the same mistake again when it came to picking a husband. The Amish way, thinking of family and community first, had to be the wisest way. Amish marriages lasted. If her father had been alive, he would have wanted her to follow in his footsteps.

Hannah had joined the Amish faith, hadn't she? She hadn't rejected it. She'd had a good marriage and a good life because she'd become Amish.

How much easier things would have been if she, Grace, had been born to Hannah and

Jonas Yoder instead of foolish Trudie Schrock. A feeling of guilt made her pause. It was unfair to judge her mother for the mistakes she'd made in her life. Trudie had tried her best. She hadn't abandoned her when she was born, and she'd never been cruel. Grace was convinced that Trudie simply hadn't been mature enough to have a baby, especially not alone, without family or friends to support her. And if Trudie had been unwise in her choice of boyfriends after Jonas, had Grace done any better?

She closed her eyes and prayed fervently. "Please, God, help me to do the right thing. Tell me what You want me to do."

But as hard as she strained to hear His answer, the only sound that came to her was the steady downpour of rain against the shingled roof and windows.

CHAPTER FIFTEEN

It was after dark Monday evening and still raining when John got back to the clinic. He pulled his truck into the triple garage and let himself in by a side door. He switched on the overhead lights and went to the supply room to refill the compartments in the back of his truck. He'd retrieved two bottles of lidocaine, a case of bandages, a package of gauze and a suture kit when he heard footsteps behind him.

"John?" his uncle called. Albert halted in the doorway and held out an oversize mug. "Nasty night out," he remarked. "Made you some herbal tea. Lemon."

"Thanks. Hold it for me until I get these in the truck, will you?" He'd hoped to slip into the house and go up to bed without running into either Uncle Albert or Gramps. He was in no mood for talking. All day he'd wrestled with his feelings about Grace, and he kept coming back to a dead end. His uncle was one of his favorite people in the world, and he deserved better than the poor company that John would be this evening.

The older man watched him for a moment. "Why don't you come to my office? I've been catching up on my reading. There's half a pepperoni pizza left."

John nodded. "Sounds good. I think I missed lunch today."

"And breakfast? Or did Grace feed you some of Hannah's blueberry pancakes before she told you she was quitting?"

John dropped the supplies onto a cardboard box on the table. "Maybe we should talk. I can do this in the morning." He followed his uncle down the hall into what had once been a spacious den in the original house.

This was a man's room, without the hint of a woman's touch: dark paneling, a rough stone fireplace, hardwood floors, bare of even a single throw rug. Two brown leather easy chairs and a small table were arranged in one half of the space; the other end of the room sported an oversize wooden desk and office chair, a fax machine/scanner and a pair of nineteenth-century oak cabinets. The walls were lined floor to ceiling with bookcases, filled to the max and overflowing onto the floor. The only decorations were three English oil paintings of hunting dogs.

John loved Uncle Albert's office. Other than the size and brand of computer, the room had barely changed since he was a boy. He paused for a few seconds, inhaling the scents of burning applewood, cold pizza and Labrador retriever. John had never entered this room without feeling the warm embrace of coming home. The familiar sensation didn't let him down tonight, and in spite of his distress about Grace, he was suddenly glad he accepted the offer of pizza and man-talk.

Travis, Uncle Albert's three-legged Lab, raised his head and thumped his tail against his sheepskin bed in greeting. "Hey, there, Trav," John said to the animal. "Flush any ducks today?" Uncle Albert never hunted, but he liked to take Travis to the marsh regularly so that the dog could swim and flush waterfowl. When John was a boy, those trips to the woods and saltwater marshes had inspired his love of wildlife photography.

John took his usual seat in the chair to the left, facing the hearth. Uncle Albert tossed Travis a biscuit and handed John the lemon tea. The three of them sat in silence for a good ten minutes while the warmth of the crackling fire and the tea drained the chill from John's muscles and bones.

It was John who broke the comfortable stillness between them. "How did you find out that Grace quit?" He hadn't wanted to talk about Grace, but so long as it was the elephant in the room, they couldn't move on to something else.

"She called in about nine o'clock. Spoke to Dad. Said you knew about it." He arched an eyebrow quizzically. "You two have a falling-out? Heard you were pretty cozy at the bazaar on Saturday."

John made a show of scowling, but it was impossible to be out of sorts with Uncle Albert. For a man who'd never married, he was surprisingly knowledgeable about women. And usually as inclined as them to gossip. Very little went on in the Mennonite or Amish communities that Uncle Albert didn't know about. He was never unkind and he was careful with whom he shared his information, but he always knew all the news before it came out in the *Budget* or the *State News*.

"We had a good time together Saturday," John agreed. "And when I told her about the chance to take the tech course, she seemed genuinely excited about the idea."

Uncle Albert opened the pizza box, which

had been standing on a section of a cherry log that did double duty as a footstool and table, and selected a generous slice. He pushed the box toward John.

John didn't bother to argue. If he refused the pizza, his uncle would remind him that he couldn't run a motor vehicle without fuel and a man was much the same. Uncle Albert was a stickler for three meals a day, no matter how irregular the fare and what time the food was consumed. John ate the pizza in silence, reserving one round of pepperoni and a bite of crust for Travis, who watched the entire process with eager anticipation.

"No begging," Uncle Albert chided.

John knew the disclaimer was just for show. His uncle would be the first to share his food with the Lab, and fortunately, despite his handicap, Travis had the metabolism of a hummingbird. No matter how much the dog ate, he never put on too much weight.

"She quit because of me," John admitted. "She knows or she's guessed how I feel about her. I guess she'd rather give up her job than be around me." And not for the first time, he wondered if he'd come on too strong . . . if he had read her wrong about returning his attraction. Guilt weighed heavily on him. If he'd hurt Grace or caused her to feel threatened, he'd done more harm than he'd guessed. That was the last thing he wanted.

"But you said she seemed interested in getting the education." Uncle Albert rubbed at his graying beard. "Hannah put the kibosh on it? Because the Amish don't approve?"

John nodded. "Grace has her heart set on being Amish."

Albert mulled over that statement for a minute. "I suppose she has her reasons."

"She does." John wasn't prepared to share with his uncle what Grace had told him about her marriage. Honestly, it wasn't Uncle Albert's business . . . or anyone else's, for that matter. "But it isn't realistic. You know her chances of becoming Amish and having it work out are —"

"Less than a snowman's chance in Hannah's oven on baking day." Uncle Albert removed a second slice of pizza and offered it to John. He shook his head, and his uncle settled back and began to eat it himself.

"When she told me she didn't want to take us up on the offer, I tried to make her see reason. I wanted to tell her how much I care about her, but she wouldn't let me. We argued, and she told me that she was quitting. That was Saturday afternoon. I had hoped that she'd change her mind once she had time to think things over. She told me not to come for her this morning."

"You did, anyway."

John nodded. "When she didn't come out, I went up to the back door. Johanna answered, told me that Grace had quit. That she wasn't going to work at the clinic. Not this morning . . . not any morning."

"How come you didn't give me a call? Let us know what was up?"

"I'm sorry. I should have, but I . . . I didn't want to . . ." He tossed the last morsel of pizza crust to Travis. "The truth is, I guess I felt as if telling you might make it real, and I didn't want it to be."

"You still have it bad for her, don't you?"

John nodded. He did, and the disagreement hadn't changed his mind one bit. He wasn't ready to give up on her. . . . The trouble was, he didn't have the faintest idea how to fix things between them. He didn't know if it was even possible and the idea made him miserable.

"Have you considered that you might be rushing into this? That you don't know Grace well at all? That a few weeks . . . even a few months' acquaintance isn't the soundest foundation for a marriage?"

John leaned forward and rested his hands

on his knees. "I can't explain how Grace makes me feel. It's . . ." He stopped and started again. "The closest I can come is to say she completes me. When I catch sight of her, the sun comes out, no matter how hard it's raining."

His uncle groaned. "It's a weakness we Hartmans have. We get our heads set on one woman, no matter how unlikely it is that we can win her, and we won't give up."

"I know I told you that I loved Miriam, but this . . . this is different."

Travis laid his head on Uncle Albert's foot. His uncle reached down to pat the dog's head and scratched behind his ears. "Just the same, I was proud of you, the way you handled losing Miriam. I was afraid it would make you end up an old bachelor like me, and I have to admit, I'm glad to see you interested in someone else."

"It's more than interest," John said. "I understand where you're coming from. If our positions were reversed, I'd be cautioning you. It does sound rash to say I feel like this about Grace when we've hardly ever been alone together." He hesitated. "What I want is a chance to see if we're right for each other."

"And what about her? How does she feel about you?"

John shook his head. "The same, I think. But she won't admit it, not to me, maybe not to herself."

"Because you're not Amish."

"Exactly. She's just being so stubborn about the whole thing. She doesn't want to give us a chance. She doesn't realize that I can give her what she's looking for. The Amish don't have a market on good, old-fashioned courting." He gestured toward himself. "I could court her."

"Take her out in your buggy?" Albert chuckled. "In your truck? Maybe take her to a frolic or two? Or a work bee?"

John nodded. "I'd like to take her to services on Sunday, let her see what our church has to offer. I want to show her what *I* have to offer."

"Grace hasn't been baptized into the Amish church yet, has she?"

"No. There's been no talk of baptism."

"Then, technically, she's not breaking any rules by dating you. So long as you two stay out of mischief."

John felt himself flush. "It isn't like that. I want to marry Grace. I want to be a father to her little boy." He paused. "She's just not seeing the situation clearly."

Uncle Albert waited, giving John time to think.

"I wish it wasn't just me pleading my case," John said. "I wish Hannah would tell her how difficult it will be for her to convert."

Uncle Albert untied one work shoe and pulled it off. He massaged his foot. "And you've talked to Hannah about this, have you?"

"No. I didn't think . . . No, I haven't. I was afraid Grace would take it the wrong way if I went behind her back to Hannah."

"Fair enough." Uncle Albert reached for the lace on his other shoe, taking his time before speaking again. "But there's nothing to keep *me* from putting a bug in Hannah's ear, is there? Letting her know you could use a little help."

"I suppose not," John answered slowly, "but —"

"But." Uncle Albert broke into a wide grin. "Everybody calls me an old busybody. Might as well have the game as have the name, don't you think?"

The following morning, Grace stood at the door of that same room and knocked. "Dr. Hartman," she called. "It's Grace Yoder. Could I speak to you?" When he answered in the affirmative, she took a deep breath and walked in. "I owe you an apology," she said. "I'm sorry. Quitting without giving notice was wrong."

Albert Hartman turned from his filing cabinet with a folder in his hand. "You've changed your mind?" he asked, not unkindly. "You'd like your job back?"

"No, sir," she answered. This was worse than she'd thought it would be. Her mouth was dry, and her stomach felt as though she'd been riding a Ferris wheel at double speed. "No . . . I . . ." She tried again. "I realized what I did was wrong — quitting on you like that. I'd like to finish out the month, to give you time to find someone else to take care of the kennels." She knotted the corner of her apron in one hand. "I don't expect you to pay me. I just don't want to leave you without help — you've all been so good to me. I'm really sorry that this hasn't worked out."

Dr. Hartman's eyes narrowed. His eyes were brown, and his expression was so like John's that she could feel her pulse racing.

"I didn't realize that you were unhappy here, Grace." He closed the drawer on the file cabinet. "We all thought you were doing an excellent job. That's why we offered you the opportunity to enter the vet tech program at Del Tech. Is that why you decided you didn't want to work here anymore?

Because we suggested you might be able to use some further education?"

"No, sir. Well, a little, maybe." She looked down at the hardwood floor, then up at him again. "Mostly, it's personal. I don't know if John told you, but I plan to join the Amish Church. The Amish aren't allowed to go to college."

He placed the file on his desk. "So you weren't interested in the program?"

"I would have been if Hannah hadn't . . ." She stopped short. "It's not fair for me to keep the job when someone else could use the opportunity to attend college. I love it here, I do, but . . ." She clasped her hands together. "But the truth is, I come in contact with too many people here. Englishers. I need to . . . *separate* myself. Be less worldly."

Dr. Hartman tapped his pen against the desk, not in an impatient way, but in a manner that she'd seen him do when he was considering treatment for one of his patients. "Are you certain that no one here, no one in particular made you feel uncomfortable?"

"Oh no," she insisted.

"Nothing John or I did to upset you?"

Grace felt her cheeks grow warm at the mention of John's name. "No, really. John's been very kind to me and to my son."

"And Hannah didn't object to him driving you home?"

Grace shook her head. "No, not at all."

"Good. Good. Tell you what," Dr. Albert said. "How about if you go ahead and continue on in the kennel until . . . let's say after the holidays. We'll just go on as we have been until I can locate a replacement for you."

"But the college? Won't someone have to register for the spring term soon?"

"Nobody else I'd take the chance on. Not at this time. We all think you're special, Grace. If it doesn't suit you, we'll just forget the whole idea." He smiled. "How is Hannah? Well?"

"Yes," Grace answered. "Busy getting ready for the school Christmas party. I understand that the children put on skits and memorize pieces. Rebecca says all the parents and younger brothers and sisters will be there. I know Dakota, my little boy, is excited about it."

"Give Hannah my best, and the girls and Aunt Jezzy. Fine woman, Jezzy Yoder. Makes a great chocolate moon pie." He waved toward the door. "I won't keep you. I'm sure you've got lots to do this morning in the kennel."

"Thank you," she said. She turned away, then back toward him. "I really am sorry for yesterday."

"I appreciate your coming back. I'm sure it wasn't easy for you. You're right, it wasn't the right way to resign your position. But you've made up for it, Grace. Not many young women would have had the nerve to come in and admit a mistake. We'll say no more about it." He offered her his hand. "Friends?"

"Yes," she agreed, shaking his hand. "Friends."

But as she walked back down the corridor to the annex that housed the kennels, she couldn't help wishing that it had been John she'd had the conversation with . . . and John who had promised to remain her friend. Losing him . . . The lump formed in her throat again. She'd been afraid of coming face to face with John after telling him that she'd quit and then not having the nerve to face him when he'd come to the house yesterday morning. She'd hurt him and probably destroyed their friendship forever.

She swallowed, trying to convince herself that it was the only way, that doing anything else would only be encouraging him — making him think that they could continue on the way they had. *Dating.* Yes, she'd ignored what was staring her right in the face. They'd been dating.

Under the circumstances, she'd done what she had to do, but there would be a price to pay. She hoped John would get over it, but she was absolutely certain that losing his friendship would leave a lasting ache in her heart.

Tuesday, Wednesday, Thursday and then Friday passed without Grace and John running into each other. If the other employees in the office wondered why she'd missed a day of work, they were kind enough not to ask. She did her job at the clinic, went home and took care of her son. In the evenings, after supper, she, her sisters, Hannah, Irwin and Aunt Jezzy all sat around the table fashioning Christmas wreaths from live greenery to sell at Spence's Market. The money from the wreaths would go to buy textbooks for the school where Hannah taught.

All day Saturday, Grace and her sisters swept and scrubbed floors and stairs, hung quilts on the clothesline to air. Even Irwin was pressed into service to wash windows and move furniture so that the girls could dust in every corner. Aunt Jezzy and Hannah kept busy in the kitchen, baking dozens of cookies, packing them into clean, shiny lard cans for Christmas and rolling dough for pie crusts. Even Miriam and Ruth came to help make the farmhouse spotless for the holidays.

After the busy day, Ruth and Miriam remained to share a light supper of potato soup and chicken salad sandwiches, but the delicious smells of roasting turkey and baking ham filled the kitchen and wafted through all the rooms. Because even a visiting Sunday was a day of rest, Saturday was the time for making baked beans, deviled eggs, scalloped potatoes, Brown Betty pudding, cranberry sauce and a counterful of pies to satisfy guests at the next day's midday meal.

As Grace bathed Dakota and tucked him into bed, she realized that she was tired, and might turn in early herself. But no matter how weary she was, she was glad that she'd felt a part of the household today. The empty place inside her, left after losing John's friendship, surely, in time, with God's help, would fill. In the days to come, she told herself, she'd find happiness in the small joys of the day: Dakota's laughter, the pleasure of a task well done, the knowledge that she was living her life as her grandparents had. She would find peace here. There was no other choice.

She returned to the kitchen to bid Hannah and the others good-night, but was surprised to find the room empty. Puzzled, Grace looked around. It wasn't quite eight o'clock. The propane lamp over the table was still burning, but there was no sign of any of her sisters. Had Miriam and Ruth left already? Aunt Jezzy never went to bed before ten, and even her rocking chair sat empty, the ever-present bag of knitting standing beside it.

"Hello?" Grace called. "Where is everyone?" She went to the back door and looked out. Still no one.

"Grace!"

She turned to see Johanna in the hallway.

"Come, sister," Johanna said. "We would speak with you."

Even more confused, Grace followed her. Johanna pushed open the parlor door, the room that was never used except to welcome important visitors. There was Hannah, Aunt Jezzy, Miriam, Ruth, Susanna, Rebecca, even Anna. They were all seated in a circle facing one empty chair. Behind them stood the men of the family: Charley, Eli, Samuel and Irwin, arms folded, expressions so

265

solemn that they might have been carved in oak.

"Sit," Johanna said, pointing to the solitary walnut chair. Miriam scooted over to make room for Johanna, and she slid in on the straight-backed settee.

"What is all this?" Grace asked.

"Sit, daughter," Hannah said.

Terrified, Grace looked from one sister to the other. "Have I done something wrong?" she demanded. "Are you sending me away?"

"Sit, child," Hannah repeated. "Open your heart and your ears and listen."

"*Ya,*" Anna said kindly. "It's time to stop trying to fit into a shoe that was made for another woman."

"Don't," Grace murmured, backing into the chair. "I'll do better. I promise."

"You can't," Johanna said softly. "No matter how much you want it, a bluebird can't turn herself into a wren."

"Please." Grace looked from Rebecca to Miriam, fearing she might burst into tears. She'd been trying so hard. How could they do this to her? "I just want to be Amish like you."

"You are my sister," Ruth said. "But you must know that you are of the world."

Susanna ran to Grace and hugged her.

266

"You are my sister," she whispered, "but you're not *Plain*."

CHAPTER SIXTEEN

"What more can I do?" Grace pleaded. Her eyelids burned, but she couldn't cry. The hurt was too deep for tears. She'd found her family, and now they were rejecting her. "I'm already quitting my job. I can't believe that —"

"Hush, child," Hannah soothed. "We need you to listen to what we have to say." She nodded to Miriam.

Miriam folded her hands in her lap and looked at Grace. "We've all been talking and . . . You need to understand that not everyone is born to wear the *Kapp.*" She shrugged. "Our way isn't the way for everyone."

The room was quiet for a moment.

"If Dat were still here, he would agree with us," Rebecca said.

Grace looked from one sister to the next.

"What we're trying to say —" it was Anna who spoke next "— is that, Grace . . . you aren't meant to be Amish."

Grace rose to her feet feeling as if her heart might break. "So that's it? You're giving up on me?"

"*Ne,*" Hannah assured her. "That's not what we're saying. Please sit." She paused. "And know that this isn't easy for us, either."

Grace sank back into her chair.

"We've all gotten the impression that you have in your head that we are something we're not," Hannah continued. "That . . . in seeking our life, you've been seeking something from God." Again, she paused. "We think this might have something to do with your past . . . before you came to us."

Grace felt her cheeks grow warm. She looked at the floor.

Aunt Jezzy spoke next. "Forgiveness comes to anyone who asks God for it, child. You *do* know that, don't you?"

Grace lowered her head to her hands. "I don't know what I know anymore."

"You know God's been with you all this time," Aunt Jezzy said. "Didn't you see His hand?"

Grace lifted her head to look at them all, not sure what to say.

"Think, Grace." It was Hannah again. "Why did you come here? *Who* guided your footsteps from so far away to this house?"

"I guess I thought God did," she answered.

"He brought you home to Seven Poplars to us, to your father's family, to your Amish roots," Hannah agreed.

Grace nodded. "But I thought He led me here so I could be Amish."

"Maybe He led you here to find us . . . but also to find a good man of faith, a man who will love you and care for you and Dakota."

Grace blinked. "A man?"

"A good husband." Rebecca smiled shyly. "It's what we all hope for, isn't it?"

Grace still didn't know where this conversation was going, but she had an idea. "But if I become Amish, I can stay with you. Be with you always. I don't want to lose you."

Susanna burst into laughter. *"Snitzeldoodle!"* She covered her mouth with her hands and giggled. "You are our sister. You can't stop being a sister. People don't stop being family."

"Susanna is right. Amish or English, you will always be a part of our family," Hannah explained.

"And you will be welcome here, in my mother's house, in any of our homes," Johanna said. "With *us.* As long as you want to stay."

"We're not turning you away," Hannah continued. "My husband's girl would always be welcome at my table. But . . ." She rose and crossed to Grace and hugged her tightly. "But we have come to love you for you, not for who your father was. For Grace Yoder, alone."

"*Ya,*" Irwin chimed in. "You're all right for an Englisher."

"I don't know what to say," Grace managed, touching her hands to her temples. She actually felt dizzy. "I . . . I was so scared. I thought you were sending me away."

"*Snitzeldoodle,*" Rebecca teased. "Susanna has it right. Our Leah is already living far from here. Mam doesn't want to lose another daughter so soon."

Grace closed her eyes for a moment, then opened them. "So . . . what am I supposed to do now? If . . . if I'm not supposed to be Amish."

"God will tell, in time." Aunt Jezzy pointed to the door. "But right now, I think you need to tend to that good man waiting in the kitchen."

Grace stared at her. A man in the kitchen? This . . . this *Amish intervention* was becoming stranger and stranger. She had thought

271

maybe Hannah was referring to John, but now she was afraid —

"Eli, would you ask him to come in?" Hannah said.

Grace half rose again and Hannah waved her back into her seat. "A man has come to see you, daughter. Sit and receive him."

Susanna giggled and whispered loudly behind her hand. "He wants to court you."

"Who wants to court me?" Grace asked. Shivers ran down her arms. *John. It had to be John. If it wasn't John, she would . . . she would run out of the room.* Relief that it was not Lemuel or some stern Amish stranger made her giddy as John appeared in the doorway.

Susanna bounced up and down with delight, clapping her hands together.

Grace said the first thing that came to her mind. "I'm sorry, John," she cried. "I was wrong. Can I have my job back?"

"Nope." John folded his arms over his chest and shook his head. "You can't. I got someone else. The scholarship is still open, though." John gazed down at her. "I'd like you to reconsider accepting it, but more importantly . . ."

"Just spit it out before she gets away," Charley urged.

John took a deep breath and squared his

shoulders.

Grace's heart did a little flip-flop as their gazes met. He looked nervous. *Why did he look so nervous?*

"Will you do me the honor of becoming my wife?" John asked. "And before you say anything, I want you to know that I'd like to adopt Dakota. I want him to legally be my son . . . *our* son."

Grace was glad she was sitting down. If she hadn't been, she knew that her knees wouldn't hold her upright. At the same time, she felt light enough to float up to the ceiling. She tried to think of something to say, but again, she was speechless.

"Say yes," Miriam urged with a giggle. *"Snitzeldoodle."*

Johanna gave her a little nudge. "He'll make a fine father for your son."

"Snap him up before Rebecca does," Ruth teased.

"I know this is sudden." John offered his hand, walking over to Grace. "Come walk with me. We'll talk."

"Don't turn him down until you hear him out," Samuel urged. "He owns land, and he's a good animal doctor. He'll be a good provider."

"And he's a man of faith." Hannah smiled at John and winked at him. "Even if he is

Mennonite."

John's strong fingers closed around Grace's. Somehow, she found the strength to rise and go with him. She was vaguely aware of his helping her into her coat, wrapping a scarf over her head and leading her outside into the chilly night air.

"Where are we going?" she asked.

"Just walking. How about the orchard?"

She nodded. She needed to get out into the crisp air to clear her head. "Yes, let's walk." She savored the warmth of his hand as she glanced back at the house. The moon was round and full and as orange as a pumpkin, making the yard almost as bright as early morning. "I'm not sure what just happened in there."

"Are you cold?" Their breaths made gray puffs of condensation in the air.

"No. I like it. It smells like Christmas, doesn't it?" The sweet, pungent scent of fresh-cut evergreens from the unfinished wreaths on tables in the backyard mingled with wood smoke. Giddy with happiness, she squeezed his hand. "They ambushed me, all of them. It was a setup and I walked right into it." She looked up at him. "And you knew, didn't you? That they were going to do this. I should be mad at you for not warning me."

"Don't blame me." John chuckled. "It was Uncle Albert who went to Hannah this week. He picked her up after school, and they hatched this up between them. Hannah told my uncle that you and I were like two goats butting our heads together. Apparently, they decided we needed some straight talk from the family."

She looked at him, suddenly remembering what Hannah had said back at the house about God's forgiveness. "Did you tell them about Joe and me? About our marriage?"

He shook his head. "It's not my place to tell. I don't know that you need ever tell anyone."

She nibbled on her lower lip. "I should tell Hannah. I think I want to," she said in a small voice.

"So tell her when you're ready."

"I thought maybe she knew. The way she was talking about God having forgiven me and led me here."

"All you have to do to be forgiven is ask."

"Hannah said the same thing," she mused.

He squeezed her hand. "Hannah's a wise woman."

She wanted to pinch herself to make sure she wasn't dreaming. When she'd walked into the parlor and saw all the family waiting, she'd been certain that her life was falling apart. Now, in the light of this beautiful moon, with John's hand in hers, with him keeping step beside her, nothing felt beyond her reach. Was it God's forgiveness that had been there all along that was making her feel this way? Was it finally forgiving herself?

"So, no more games between us, Grace," John said. "I love you, and I think you love me, even if you don't realize it yet. And I want you to be my wife." He went on before she had a chance to argue. "You're one of a kind, Grace. It was no accident that we met, and no accident that I haven't been able to think of anyone else since I laid eyes on you."

"Hannah said that," she mused. "She said that if God led me to Seven Poplars, he might have been leading me to you all along."

"Sounds right to me."

Grace walked beside him, feeling his breath in sync with hers. She was in love with him. She really was. "I don't know how to explain it to you, how alone I've felt all my life. Even when I was with Joe, I still felt like I was alone."

"You'll never be alone again. You have me, and you have a family to watch over you. They love you, Grace. Hannah and your sisters and their husbands."

They walked in silence past the barn and the corral, past the brick structure of an old well and a root cellar. The hard-packed dirt lane curved around Johanna's turkey run and led into the orchard. They were beneath the spreading apple trees when John stopped and spoke again.

"Hannah warned me that if I didn't do right by you, I'd have to answer to her." He turned to her, lifted her hand to his lips and gently kissed the tops of her knuckles. "It isn't our custom to wear rings, but if you want one, I'll buy you one."

"No, I don't need a ring. My sisters don't wear one." She looked into his eyes. "But I haven't said *yes,* yet, John Hartman. Don't get your cart before the horse. Susanna said you wanted to court me, and I think I like that idea."

"Just what Uncle Albert said. He thought I should state my intentions, and then we should walk out together, Amish-style." He chuckled. "It seems that that's the way we've already been doing this. I mean, I already drove you home from a frolic in a buggy."

She giggled. "In a hay wagon, not a buggy." She took a breath. "John, this is all crazy. We've got to be crazy. We've known each other only three and a half months.

What do you know about me?"

"That I want to know you better." They started walking again, now arm in arm. "That I've never met anyone who makes me feel the way you do."

"Are you sure this isn't too soon to talk of marriage?" she asked.

"I'm asking you to commit to a betrothal and then take all the time you need to be certain I'm right for you," he answered, and the deep timbre of his voice made her shiver with excitement. "We'll marry when you're ready. Three months or three years from now, that's up to you."

"You may change your mind about marrying me when you find out that I can't cook."

"That makes two of us who can't cook. So, either one of us learns or we live on takeout pizza and Hannah's pity."

She ran her hand down his arm. "Be serious, John. They wouldn't let me be Amish. What if I can't be Mennonite, either?"

"I don't think that will be an issue. It's different with us. With Mennonites. If you come to church with me, if you decide that my faith feels right to you, then you could be baptized there. And I can promise you that you'll be welcomed with open arms. The Mennonites aren't closed off from the world. We believe in doing what we can to bring God's word and comfort to everyone who wants it."

"Like Leah and Daniel in South America."

John nodded. "But I've not been called to mission. At least not yet. I'm content to work in our community, here in Kent County. I want to be the best vet I can be, and I hope we can find time to support my church's charities, especially those that serve children."

"And you think that there would be a place for me?" She slid her hand into his, looking up at him, again. "That I could help?"

"I know you could."

She glanced away into the distant darkness. "It seems like a dream come true, that we could be together, the three of us, and that I'd still have Hannah and my sisters. It's almost too much to hope for."

He stopped and pushed the scarf back from her forehead. "Look around you, Grace, at this orchard. The apples have all been picked and the leaves have fallen, but in a few months, new leaves will form, buds will become blossoms and then bushels and bushels of delicious apples. Maybe our love is like that. It's winter now. We know what's coming in spring, or we think we do. If it would ease your heart, we can take it one day at a time. We can ride in Charley's buggy, attend services together and wait and pray for those new leaves and buds to blossom."

"Betrothed." She smiled up at him. "I think I like the taste of that word on my tongue. John Hartman . . . my betrothed." And, in spite of herself, tears began to spill down her cheeks.

"What's wrong?" he asked. "Why are you crying?"

"Happiness," she whispered. "Because . . . because . . . while nothing I planned worked out, all my dreams are coming true."

John lowered his head and brought his lips close enough to hers that she could feel the warmth of his breath on her face.

"Is that a *yes*, Grace Yoder? Will you do me the honor of becoming my wife? To have and to hold, so long as we both shall live?"

"*Ya*," she murmured softly. And then he wrapped his strong arms around her and kissed her tenderly. And she knew instantly that at long last, she'd found her way home.

Epilogue

Kent County, ten months later

Grace pulled her car into the driveway and parked under the old Sheepshead apple tree. Ripe fruit rolled and crunched under her feet as she opened the back door and scooped up her books and a bag of groceries she'd picked up on her way home. Glancing at her watch, she let herself into the mudroom with her key.

She kicked off her clogs and walked through the swinging doors into the spacious kitchen. As whenever she entered the new house, a rush of disbelief swept over her. The log house had been completed in September, two months after she and John had been married in the small, white frame Mennonite Church a few miles down the road, the same church where she'd been baptized. No matter how many times she went out of the house and came back in, seeing the warm hominess of the beautiful log cabin still thrilled her. The house John had built for her . . . *for them.*

She dropped the bag of groceries and her books on the counter and gazed around the great room that featured bare beams, reclaimed barn-wood flooring and a massive stone fireplace. "I must be dreaming," she said to the tabby cat curled up in a basket on the hearth. "I'm afraid I'll wake up and find myself back in the trailer park with a refrigerator that doesn't keep Dakota's milk cold and a stove with one working burner."

Cat, wisely, said nothing but purred in understanding. Cat had seen tough times, as well. Susanna had rescued him from two English boys at Spence's who were attempting to drown the half-starved creature in a bucket of rainwater. Cat had come out of the ordeal with a broken tail, one missing tooth and a tattered ear. Uncle Albert had soon healed her wounds, and sweet John had brought her home to live out her days in the cabin beside the pond.

Grace pulled a sweater on over her dress, turned on the oven and retrieved a family-size chicken potpie from the cloth grocery bag. She had time to stick dinner in the oven and start assembling a salad before she had to run over to Hannah's to pick up Dakota.

Hannah had been true to her word and been supportive, even when Grace had confessed that her marriage to Joe hadn't been real. The whole family had kept their promise, and a year after her arrival in Seven Poplars, Grace felt more like one of the Yoders than ever.

She glanced at the kitchen clock, wondering if she could squeeze in a shower before going for Dakota. Tonight was Wednesday prayer meeting, and Dakota's Bible school class would be packing boxes of school supplies, toys and sandals for Leah's mission school. They had to be there by seven and she wasn't sure how long the frozen potpie would take to bake. She searched for the directions on the back of the box and was about to rip open the packaging when she heard Dakota's voice at the front door.

"Mam!"

She hurried into the great room in time to lean over and catch her son as he hurled himself into her arms.

"Mam! Mam!" he cried. "We're going to do a play at school! A Christmas play. I'm going to be a sheep herd!"

"A *sheep herd*? That's wonderful," Grace exclaimed. She met John's gaze as he walked in the front door carrying their son's little backpack in one hand, a basket in the other.

"Dakota's going to be a sheep herd," she repeated.

"I think that's a *shepherd.*" John set the large wicker basket and the backpack on the counter and glanced down at the frozen potpie. "You can put that in the freezer. Hannah sent chicken and dumplings, biscuits and green beans with pecans."

"Bless her." Grace sighed. "She remembered that it was my busiest day of the week."

"Don't knock Wednesdays," he teased. "I had a good day and got off in time to pick up Dakota."

"Mam! Mam!" Dakota jumped up and down. "Jonah and me caught the black hen — the one with the white tail feathers that laid her eggs on the buggy seat."

John grinned, looking at her. "How was your day? Did you get your grade on the test?"

"Ninety-four."

"That's my girl." He put his arms around her and kissed her.

For a few seconds, Grace forgot her grade point average, forgot that dinner would be rushed and forgot that her son was telling her about an escaped hen. Nothing mattered but her dear husband and her sweet son.

When she and John separated, she was laughing and breathless. "And tomorrow we're learning to put in IVs," she managed.

John arched a dark brow. "Hopefully, you had the good sense not to mention to your instructor that you've been doing them since you were fourteen."

"I didn't." She ruffled Dakota's hair as he shot past her, taking his backpack with him.

"I'll make you a deal," John said. "You jump in the shower and Dakota and I can set the table for supper."

"And what do you get in return? Husband of the Year award?"

John's grin widened. "A happy wife makes for a happy house."

"Is this a happy house?" she asked him, taking a step toward him.

"Are you a happy wife?"

Her answer was to stand on tiptoes and kiss him again. "Couldn't be happier," she whispered. "Not even in my dreams."

Dear Reader,

Welcome to Seven Poplars, Delaware, home of the Old Order Amish family, the Yoders, and their friends and family. Grace's story came as a surprise, not only to Hannah and her daughters, but to me, as well. The joy of writing is much like life. We never know what's around the next corner. I never expected a mysterious stranger to show up at Hannah's farmhouse on a rainy night and throw the entire community into turmoil. And for the Yoders' dear friend, veterinarian John Hartman, life becomes suddenly more intriguing as he meets the tough little widow with a checkered past.

Can people change their lives by faith and determination? When we seek happiness, can we fail to see that the answer to our prayers is right in front of our eyes? When Grace announces that she wants to become Amish, life will never be the same for Hannah and her daughters. And when John decides to come between Grace and her dream, anything can happen.

I hope you'll come to love Grace as much as I have and that you'll join me again when a man from Johanna's past sets out to win her love and hand in marriage. Will he prevail or will Johanna's stubborn independence extinguish the romance before it has a chance to blossom?

Wishing you peace and joy,
Emma Miller

QUESTIONS FOR DISCUSSION

1. When Grace appeared on Hannah's doorstep and claimed to be her husband's child, what prompted Hannah to welcome her into her home rather than turning her away? Do you think finding out about Grace changed Hannah's opinion of her late husband?

2. Hannah hasn't remarried since Jonas's death, a break from Amish tradition. Why do you think she hasn't? By not remarrying, has Hannah's example made Johanna less willing to seek another husband?

3. What do you believe was Grace's primary reason for seeking her father? Do you think that the mainstream twenty-first-century American lifestyle has lost some of the family and community ties that sustain us? Do you believe that Hannah

and her daughters will remain close to Grace in the years to come?

4. Is it more difficult to be a child today than fifty years ago? Is it more difficult to be a parent? Do you believe that the complexity of American life makes it more difficult to impart morals and faith to children?

5. What is the greatest appeal the Amish way of life holds for Grace? Do you believe her rootless lifestyle causes her to idealize the Amish faith? If she hadn't met John, do you think she could have become Amish, accepted the rules of church and community, and been happy?

6. John has strong beliefs in the values of his faith, and he is active in the Mennonite Church. Do you believe that these qualities will make him a better husband to Grace and father to her son? Do you think that John would have been happy if he'd married someone without an equally strong faith?

7. John and Grace have known each other for only a few months. Do you believe that it is possible to truly know a person in

such a short time? Would you have advised them to have a long engagement?

8. Do you think Grace is partially responsible for Joe's deception concerning his marriage to her? Can you understand why she would feel so guilty about Dakota's birth? Do you think she will tell Dakota the truth when he is older?

9. Grace believes that God will forgive her if she joins her father's Amish faith, repents of her lifestyle and lives by the church rules. Do you think that was God's plan or Grace's? Have you ever struggled with knowing what God wants you to do?

10. Do you think Grace chose John because she was following her heart? Do you think they will be happy together? Do you believe Grace will find peace in the Mennonite faith?

ABOUT THE AUTHOR

Emma Miller lives quietly in her old farmhouse in rural Delaware amid fertile fields and lush woodlands. Fortunate enough to be born into a family of strong faith, she grew up on a dairy farm, surrounded by loving parents, siblings, grandparents, aunts, uncles and cousins. Emma was educated in local schools, and once taught in an Amish schoolhouse much like the one at Seven Poplars. When she's not caring for her large family, reading and writing are her favorite pastimes.